"*No Blood Spilled* is a delight: Bram Stoker meets Steven Spielberg in a fast-paced, go-for-the-jugular joyride.

"Les Daniels writes to scare; his vampire would *never* sit for an interview. Once bitten, you'll become, like me, an avid reader of this series."

—Douglas E. Winter, editor of *Prime Evil*

**THE MOON WAS A WHITE SLIVER IN THE SKY,** and Sarala was bathed in its glow, but the panther was invisible in shadows as black as its hide. He wondered how long it had been since either he or Sarala had moved . . .

A figure stepped into the clearing. The panther hissed, and snarled, and gave a grating roar, but then turned suddenly silent. Callender thought that he could hear it moving toward the black shape of a man, and then there came a low rumbling sound which he could only describe as purring.

He felt as though he had been struck in the stomach with a cannonball. He did not need to wait until the man stepped into the moonlight, with the great cat at his side rubbing against him like a pet. Before he saw the dead face he was shouting at the sky: "Newcastle!"

"A ruthless and pitiless vampire who yet elicits the reader's sympathy (or, at any rate, respect) by the cynical dignity of his bearing and his quest for knowledge."

—S.T. Joshi, *Studies in Weird Fiction*

**Tor Books by Les Daniels**

*No Blood Spilled*
*Yellow Fog*

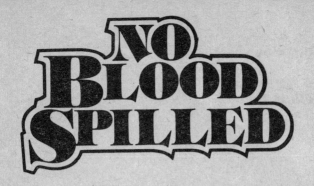

# NO BLOOD SPILLED

## LES DANIELS

TOR HORROR

A TOM DOHERTY ASSOCIATES BOOK
NEW YORK

This is a work of fiction. All the characters and events portrayed in this book are fictitious, and any resemblance to real people or events is purely coincidental.

NO BLOOD SPILLED

Copyright © 1991 by Les Daniels

A Tor Book
Published by Tom Doherty Associates, Inc.
49 West 24th Street
New York, N.Y. 10010

Cover art by Duncan Eagleson

ISBN: 0-812-50932-3

First edition: February 1991

Printed in the United States of America

0  9  8  7  6  5  4  3  2  1

# Contents

# *O N E*

# *The Man in the Cage*

The madman sat in his cell and dreamed of death.

He dreamed of his own death, which he tried not to wish for, and he dreamed of the death of others. One was the woman he had hoped to marry, and one was the man responsible for killing her, a man he knew had been a corpse for centuries.

This conviction had led the courts to declare Reginald Callender mad, a decision that had saved his life and then sent him straight to hell.

He listened to the screams of the damned around him and decided to try standing again. His feet were sore and the muscles in his legs throbbed painfully, but he was determined to sit as little as possible, and never to lie down at all in the filth that covered the floor. Much of this, it shamed and sickened him to know, had come from his own body; he had been chained here for more than a week.

He struggled upward into a squat, bracing his back

1

against the rough stone wall behind him, hearing the jangle of his chains and the squealing scrape of the iron band around his waist as it rubbed against wet rock. The waist band was hardly an annoyance now, since he had grown so thin, but the smaller ring around his neck was agony, half strangling him and rubbing his flesh raw. Both restraints were chained to the wall, but he had slack enough to move for a few feet, except for those times that he could not bear to think about. He moved as slowly and silently as he could, desperate not to draw attention to himself. He never even screamed anymore, except of course when the chains grew suddenly shorter.

Reginald Callender finally reached his feet, a good night's work for any man in this forsaken hole. All but winded by his exertions, he gasped for breath and inhaled the foul stew of damp, decay, and his own stench that filled the cell. He listened to his teeth chattering, and a cold chill ran through him that set his chains to rattling again. He cradled his body in his thin arms and attempted to distract himself by thinking of McNaughten once again.

If not for McNaughten, Reginald Callender would have been in his grave. Not that he was far from it, trapped in a cell that was hardly longer than a coffin and even deeper underground. There was little to be thankful for in this existence except that it might someday provide an opportunity for escape, and for revenge, and for at least such happiness as that would bring; and this was reason enough for Callender to love McNaughten, whom he had never met, as he would love a brother.

An older brother, to be sure, for McNaughten had been the first man in England to be convicted as a murderer and then spared the gallows because he was mad. That had been four years ago, in 1843, when McNaughten had killed the secretary of the man who headed Scotland Yard, Sir

2

Robert Peel. This deed itself was enough to endear McNaughten to his spiritual successor, who had come to hate the police with a passion, but McNaughten's greatest gift had been to be so utterly insane that even the courts had been compelled to notice it. Callender remembered the decision as if it were a litany: "The party accused was laboring under such a defect of reason, from disease of the mind, as not to know the nature and quality of the act he was doing."

A precedent, that's what the lawyers called it; McNaughten didn't hang, and so Callender didn't either. He wondered how McNaughten was enjoying life. And he remembered how he had enjoyed it himself, so few years ago, when he had sat in the Commerce Club beside an open fire, a drink in one hand and the London *Times* in the other, denouncing the decision that had let a murderer go free.

Free! Callender rattled his chains and laughed. He stifled the sound at once, praying that it would be lost among the sobs and catcalls and obscenities that echoed down the asylum's clammy corridors. The best policy was to be inconspicuous; the keepers didn't like him at the best of times. They shared the widespread delusion that he had murdered the lovely young woman that he should have wed, when in fact, of course, he had only meant to kill the monster who was threatening her, the monster they would not believe existed. He held his breath, peered into the corners of his cell, and whispered the word into the darkness.

"Vampire."

The high walls outside Halliwell House were black against the clear sky of a winter night as Nigel Stone paced back and forth in front of them. He wondered if it would snow in time for Christmas. He wondered if he should forget about his business here and go home to his wife.

He wondered if this was just a fool's errand or actually a lunatic's. He looked up and saw that, sure enough, the moon was full.

"Blast!" he said.

He was a lunatic, no doubt of it, planning to bribe his way into an asylum to see a man he wished he could forget. Yet somehow, all these weeks after the trial, he could not erase the picture of Reginald Callender from his mind. It might have been because they were cousins; it might even have been because despite himself he wondered if his cousin might just possibly be telling the truth. A man who has spent ten years in India learns the value of believing almost anything.

He might even believe in Christmas, which was coming soon, and so take pity on his fellow man. This bleak neighborhood on the outskirts of London displayed nothing that might remind a visitor of Christmas, and the grim bulk of Halliwell House showed no signs of pity. It was up to Nigel Stone to do what he could, even if it meant paying a call on a murderer.

He pounded on the wooden door in the wall with his gloved fist, then stamped his feet on the pavement to ward off the cold. He watched his breath billow out in front of him like cigar smoke, then struck his fist against the door again. A panel swung open and a sharp, unshaven face poked out.

"What do you want, then? Be quiet! Go away! You don't want to come in here!"

"But I do, my dear fellow. Don't you remember me?"

The man behind the wall squinted at Stone. He held up a lantern. "Oh," he said. "You're the fat one."

"I don't see that my figure enters into the matter," huffed Stone. "You told me to come back at night, and then you'd let me in."

"I said I might, that's all. I shouldn't. It isn't proper.

4

They passed a law, you know. We're not supposed to let the gentry in to look at the loonies.''

"But I don't want to look at anyone, my good man. I just want to see my cousin."

"Well, what's the difference, then? It's still unlawful.''

The two men stared at each other through the opening in the door: Stone baffled, the turnkey waiting for the light of reason to dawn at last. A few seconds passed.

"Look here," Stone finally said. "How much will it cost me to get through this door?"

"Oh, I wouldn't like to say, sir." The gatekeeper looked his prospect up and down, trying to assess the cut of his clothes. There was another pregnant pause. "Half a crown," he said.

"Done!" said Stone, reaching into his pocket with such alacrity that the man behind the wall cursed himself as an easy mark. Still, a bargain was a bargain. He shuffled through the keys on his steel ring, selected the largest, and turned it in the lock. When the door was opened, he pulled Stone through and locked it behind him, then sat down on a three-legged stool and fished a pipe out of his pocket. "There you are, sir," he said.

"There I am?" echoed Stone. "Where am I?"

He looked across a barren stretch of ground toward a gloomy old mansion with bars on all its windows, only one of which showed any light. Then he looked at his host, wrapped in a bedraggled greatcoat and smoking his pipe under a dead tree.

"See here," said Stone. "This won't do at all. I told you I had to get in there to see my cousin."

"No, sir. You asked me how much it would cost to get through that door there. And now you're through."

"And you told me it was a crime to let me in, didn't you? You just might find yourself up on a report before

5

morning, unless you take me to see Mr. Callender at once.''

The gatekeeper examined his visitor with new interest. On the surface, he was just a red-faced, middle-aged gent with jowls and a befuddled attitude, but there was apparently a bit of the bulldog in him.

The turnkey sighed and stood up. He knocked his pipe against his boot and ground its glowing embers into the dirt. He picked up his lantern. ''George won't like it,'' he said. ''Most likely he'll throw you out.''

''George? And who is George?''

''The head keeper, that's George. He runs the place at night. Used to be a prizefighter. Not a pleasant fellow, George. Not a bit like me. He might break your head. He might break mine. He likes breaking things, does George. And if he doesn't kill us both, he'll charge you more than half a crown to let you in. If he lets you in at all.''

''You should have arranged things with him.''

''Oh, I did, sir, but he was sober then.''

The man with the lantern led the way surefootedly up the broken steps of Halliwell House, not even hesitating at the sound of an unearthly wail that stopped Stone dead. ''My God! What was that?''

''Might be your cousin, for all I know. Him or one of his little friends. Just come through here, sir.''

''Shouldn't the house be locked?'' asked Stone as he stepped into its dusty entrance hall.

''No need, really. The children are all safe in their rooms, and there's more than one way to make sure they stay. For one thing, they'd have to get past George. Come on.''

Stone followed his guide down the empty hallway toward a double door, which just as they reached it burst open with a crash, both doors banging into the walls. A

6

gigantic figure, silhouetted by the firelight behind it, lumbered forward. "Who's there?" a hoarse voice bellowed.

Stone took three quick steps backward, but the gatekeeper was not so quick. A hand the size of a ham shot out and clutched him by the collar.

"It's me, George, it's only me! You know me!"

The giant pulled his prey back into the light.

"You!" he roared. "What are you sneaking around here for?"

"I wasn't sneaking, George, honest I wasn't! I came to visit, that's all. Me and this gentleman. He's got money for you, George!"

The head keeper relaxed his grip. He thought for a moment. "You get back outside," he said, and his underling scurried away.

He looked at Stone, and Stone looked at him. The head keeper was a mountain of muscle, not much of it gone to fat, and not more than an inch under seven feet tall. His nose had been broken and flattened, his ears were twisted lumps of cartilage, and his eyes were crisscrossed with broken blood vessels. His head was shaved except for a black stubble, and he reeked of gin.

"You come in here," he said.

Nigel Stone moved forward gingerly, careful to give no offense. He stepped into a small anteroom, which seemed to contain nothing but a fireplace, an armchair, and a small table supporting a bottle of gin. The man called George lumbered toward the fire, then turned around with a heavy brass poker in his hand. Stone moved away from him and the keeper smiled.

"Afraid, are you? You don't have to be afraid of me. It's them you have to be afraid of." He jerked a thumb toward a small door opposite the entrance to his lair. He squatted to stir up the fire, his eyes darting from left to

7

right, then leaped up and hurled the poker across the room. Stone threw himself out of the way as it clattered into a dark corner.

"Rats," George explained. He smiled again, showing the few teeth he still possessed. "They're everywhere. Can't get rid of 'em, but I can put the fear of God into 'em, eh?"

He sat in his chair and emptied a good quarter of the gin bottle into his mouth, then threw his head back and swallowed. "Now," he said. "What do you want here?"

Nigel Stone knew he should disguise his nervousness, but didn't know if he could do it. "I've come to see a man," he said as firmly as he could. His voice only broke on the first word.

"What man?"

"His name is Callender."

"You want to see Callender? A gent like you? He's not a pretty sight. Go home."

"He's my cousin."

"He's a murderer. He killed a girl. Shoved something right through her, that's what I heard."

"His cane," said Nigel Stone. George looked thoughtful.

"I won't ask why you want to see him," he said. "Maybe you want to kill him. We've had 'em disappear before, you know. Nobody wants 'em. This isn't even a government asylum. This is a private house. We get the worst ones here, contracted out, you might say, to a place where's there's no rules and no reforms. And no inspectors. We use the old ways, and we don't cost the treasury much. We just keep 'em here until they die, and they die soon."

"Then I must see Reginald Callender at once."

"Before he dies, you mean?"

8

"I mean so that he will not die at all."

"That's not so easy to arrange as the other way around," said George. Still seated in his chair, he leaned over so that his back was turned toward Stone and began to fool with something near the floor. Stone could see the man's muscles working under his coat, and he could hear the sound of metal scraping.

"What are you doing there?" he demanded.

The keeper stood and faced him, laughing silently. "Just making sure that he's awake, that's all."

"Then you'll take me to him?"

"Aye. For a pound."

Stone started to argue, recalled that his wife had made him a rich man, and handed over the money. George produced a lantern and lit it with a piece of kindling from the fire. "You'll have to carry that," he told Stone. "I need one hand for the keys, and the other one for this."

George held up a whip as long as he was tall.

"That thing's for horses, not for men," said Stone.

"I never knew a horse that was a murderer. Come on."

Stone followed the man called George through the small door against the back wall, but almost at once he wished he hadn't. The stench alone was enough to discourage anyone. They walked through a dark passageway, where the lantern Stone carried sent their ugly shadows jumping against the cobwebbed walls, their surfaces damp with mold, fungus, and decay. Below them was a stone stairway.

As they shuffled down it, Stone listened to the sounds. They were human, technically, yet so grotesque and obscene that he wanted to turn around. At the foot of the stairs, where the noises were louder, he finally stopped.

"Listen!" he said. "What's down here?"

"Your cousin," answered George. "You can still go

9

home now if you've changed your mind. You can't have that pound back, though.''

"Just keep going," Stone said with all the enthusiasm he could muster. They turned into a hall that was more like a tunnel, its ceiling so low that the gigantic keeper and even the more compactly constructed Stone had no choice but to bend double as they crept forward into utter blackness; George's squatting bulk blocked out all sight of what might lie ahead. Stone began to feel like he was in a trap, and it did nothing to raise his spirits when he realized that the din of pleas and curses and catcalls had now surrounded him. He glanced nervously at the low, locked doors on either side of him, each one fixed with a small grate from which he half expected eager hands to reach. He realized that the lantern had almost fallen from his fingers, and he took a firmer grip on it when he heard George speak.

"This should be the one. Put the light down on the ground and stand away.''

Stone took a few steps back and watched the keeper fumbling with his keys before a door that looked as if it might have been designed for a small child. Suddenly Nigel Stone was struck by the queasy notion that his cousin might have been transformed, through surgery or sorcery, into some small, misshapen thing. He was not reassured when the door opened and a little laughter trickled out.

"Are you receiving visitors this evening, sir?" asked George as he thrust his shaven head halfway into the shadowed opening. The only reply was a faint shuffling, yet George lifted his head up with a broad smile and told Stone to go in.

"In there, you mean?''

"That's right, just crawl on in. You can take the lantern with you.''

Stone felt himself shudder, and the shame of that sent him moving toward that ominously low door. He realized he really would have to crawl through. He carried the light in front of him, determined at least to see what he was getting in for, and crept through mud upon his hands and knees. His first thought, as he snaked his head into the hole, was that the air alone would kill him; his second thought was that he must have come to the wrong place. The thing in front of him could not be Reginald Callender.

Then all thought rushed away as he was kicked and shoved into the monster's lair. The door slammed shut behind him and the key clicked in the lock.

Stone whirled as best he could in his uncomfortable position and banged both hands against the door. "What are you doing there?" he shouted.

"I'm sure you want a private interview," said the rough voice from outside, "and I can't afford to leave things open, now, can I?"

"Let me out at once," screamed Stone, and he heard voices much like his from down the hall.

"You sound like you belong here, don't you, sir? But never worry, I'll be back to get you soon. That's if I don't forget, of course."

Stone managed to suppress another scream, even when he heard the sound of a man walking away. Instead he looked over his shoulder at what seemed to be hanging from the wall. It made that noise that might have been a laugh.

"Not very pleasant here, is it?"

The voice, however dry and cracked, was unmistakable. "Reggie! That is you!"

The man on the wall, just visible in the lantern's misdirected glare, resembled one of the filthy beggars Stone had seen in India. Actually he looked more like a corpse,

11

but corpses never spoke and never moved. Reginald Callender, once as elegant a dandy as Victorian London ever saw, slumped in chains and rags. His wild hair and patchy beard almost obscured his face, but his tattered clothes revealed how pale and gaunt he had become. He was covered with more filth than fabric, and fresh blood trickled from the iron band around his neck. His eyes just stared. Stone held the light up to him and stared back.

"Aren't you glad to see me, Cousin Nigel?"

"I'd be glad to get out of here, that's all. But I did come, didn't I? Wanted to see how you were, Reggie. It's been months, after all. It's almost Christmas."

"Christmas!" echoed Callender. "Did you bring me a gift?"

"A gift? I never thought of such a thing, old man. I mean to say, what could I bring to you in here?"

"Food. Did you bring any food?"

"Oh. I see what you mean," said Stone, realizing with a chill that his cousin had become a beggar in more than appearance. "I'm afraid I never thought of it. Didn't really expect to see you like this. After all, isn't this some sort of hospital?"

"You see what sort it is," croaked Callender, looking on with bitter amusement as his cousin went through his pockets as if he actually hoped to find a pie or a slice of beef somewhere in his clothing. Then Stone's face lit up.

"Cigars!" he said. "I've got some cigars. And I've got a little flask of brandy! What do you think of that?"

"Let me have it," Callender barked, shuffling forward as far as the chains that held him at waist and neck would let him move. Stone wanted to retreat from the sinister figure, but he stood his ground and held out the silver flask. Callender snatched it from him with trembling fingers, fumbled to open it, put it to his crusted lips, then pulled it away untasted.

"I can't," he whispered. "I mustn't. That's what got me here. I must keep my mind clear."

"Go on, Reggie. There's only a little. I know you were having a bit much in the old days, but it's so cold and damp down here. It'll do you good. And take my greatcoat, too. You need it more than I do."

Callender looked at him oddly from the corner of one eye, then took a long drink while the heavy coat was wrapped around his scrawny shoulders. He felt the old familiar warmth spread through his system, and the thick garment stopped his shivering. He was beginning to feel almost human again. "You're a good fellow, cousin," he said.

Stone huffed with embarrassment and slipped a fine cigar into Callender's mouth. He was just about to light it when suddenly his cousin was flung across the cell and back into the far wall, just like a man who had been shot with a powerful gun. Stone heard the impact of flesh against rock and watched his cousin fall face-first into the muck below. There had been no sound of a shot, only a metallic rattle that Stone thought he recognized.

"Reggie! God! What's happened?" He rushed to the stricken man's side, almost convinced that he had seen something uncanny. Callender was still breathing, but gasping and choking like a man who had been strangled. He lifted his head, and Stone saw bright blood trickling from the iron band around his neck.

"They've been pulling my chain again," Callender whispered when he could finally speak.

"Pulling your chain?"

"It's a form of discipline, they say, and also a form of

13

entertainment. That creature George did it to me just before you came down.''

Stone thought back to a scene upstairs and cringed. He held up the lantern and saw that his cousin's chains were not attached to the wall, but rather ran through it to a place he could not see but could now well imagine.

"This is monstrous!" said Nigel Stone.

"I haven't been a model prisoner," said Callender. "But never mind about that now. He may be back in a few minutes. Tell me what you know about Newcastle."

"Newcastle?"

"Mr. Sebastian Newcastle, or Don Sebastian de Villanueva, or whatever name you choose to call him by. What has become of him?"

"The one you said was a vampire?"

"The one who tricked me into committing murder."

"He's gone. The police wanted to question him about your case, but there was no sign of him. And yet I wonder if I don't know what's become of him. It's mad, of course . . . Oh, sorry . . .''

"Tell me what you mean. Quickly!"

"After all that happened . . . after you were arrested, there was a big box in your house, a crate. It was in your hall, addressed as if you meant to ship it out. I thought it might be business, and I meant to help you, so I had it shipped. It went to India. Calcutta. I wasn't really thinking then, what with that poor girl dead and you in prison, but I think it was addressed to that man Newcastle."

"You fool," said Callender quietly. "You let him escape."

"It couldn't have been anything. It was just a box."

"He was inside it! I know he was! You told me you'd heard of such things when you were in India yourself."

"You mean some trick of a fakir, some kind of yogi trance?"

"I mean a living corpse."

"If I believed that, old fellow, I'd be in the cell beside you. You mustn't think of such things."

"Never mind that now. My keeper will be here soon." Callender groped in the filth beneath him for the silver flask and drained it dry. "Take this with you," he said, "and take the coat as well. They'd only be stolen."

"This treatment is abominable," said Stone. "I'll take it up with the authorities!"

"Don't do that! I'd pay for it. If you want to help me, you must bribe the man who brought you here. Money's the only thing they understand. I was that way myself not long ago. Give him whatever you can, Nigel, I beg of you. And tell him you'll be back again to see what has become of me. You will come back?"

"As soon as I can get away. In a few days, before Christmas. And you buck up, my lad. I won't forget you."

Callender would have said more, but he saw the door to his cell open before his cousin did.

"Had a nice visit, gentlemen?" asked George.

Callender put a warning finger to his lips, and Stone kept silent until he was out of the cell with the lantern. Then Callender could hear his cousin's voice rising in the huff and puff of protest, until it woke the other prisoners and was drowned in the roar of their insanity.

And in the midst of their cacophony, Reginald Callender leaned back against his wall and smiled. It was a long voyage to India, but not half as long as the distance between this hideous hole and the streets of London.

Still, Callender thought, there just might be a way.

# TWO

# The Man in the Box

The man in the box floated among the faint sounds of the sea, waiting once again for night to fall. He was starving, so weak that soon he would not be able to set himself free from his wooden prison, yet attempting to escape now would doom him undeniably, for he was adrift in unknown waters.

The box was full of darkness, and it was damp, but it had been so skillfully constructed that no water could penetrate its shell; it drifted on the surface like an airborne seed in search of fertile soil.

The box was a coffin.

The painstaking English cabinetwork that had gone into its construction proved to be well worth the expense it had entailed, although only an Englishman could have explained why it was worthwhile to keep a corpse hermetically sealed, and to deny that decay was death's handmaiden. Still, to a man who was not exactly dead in

16

the conventional sense, a coffin of such perfect workmanship was a pearl beyond price.

Of course he had hardly expected to use it as a boat, but then neither had he anticipated the typhoon that had, two nights ago, destroyed the ship on which he sailed. This was to have been the last leg of a long journey from London to Calcutta, a voyage so uneventful that he had grown complacent. With the coffin hidden in a crate, and the crate buried in the cargo hold, there was little danger of discovery; his nocturnal visits to members of the crew were so discreet that not one man had died. Too late now to wish that he had gorged himself on their bright blood; their bloated bodies lay scattered uselessly upon the ocean floor, food only for the fishes and whatever other creatures lurked below. Worse yet, he might soon be among them, and most certainly would be unless he found a way to reach the shore.

The waves which bore the coffin on their ebb and swell were part of the Bay of Bengal, of that much he was certain. And the ship, traveling northeast from Madras to Calcutta, had no doubt hugged the coastline to its west, but who could say how far the storm had carried him? He might be hundreds of miles from the nearest land, with no way of telling in what direction it might lie. So he had hoped to let fortune and the tides decide his fate, but tonight would be his last chance to act.

When the sun had set, he would abandon the coffin and set his sights on the sky. He had strength enough for one last metamorphosis, and as a winged explorer of the night he might meet with the refuge that he sought. If not, the dawn would make short work of him, wings plummeting in flame toward one last death, but still the struggle was the better choice, better than the slow starvation which would leave him trapped in a helpless body for eternity.

There was another chance as well, for when the darkness fell, he might look out across the endless sea and spy its end, a dark shore where he could return to earth at last, to the deep earth that nourished and sheltered him. For the earth teemed with life, while in all of the vast ocean there was only death for him.

Yet there he dreamed and drifted, the memories of centuries long past washing over him like the gray-green waves that bore him aloft.

He waited.

The waters were as deep and dark as the eyes of the boy who looked out over them. He was called Jamini, and he might have been twelve years old, but there was nobody to let him know for sure. The men who had found him in the streets some years ago, who fed him when there was food and struck him when there was not, were his only family, his only teachers, his only friends. He was not certain if they were training him to be a fisherman or a thief, but both were pleasant trades despite the risk and the uncertainty. The men owned nothing of any value except the boat on which they sailed, and most of the time it was their home as well.

The boat, a dinghy about thirty feet in length, skimmed over the surface like a quarter-moon that had dropped down into the sea, the curved stern higher than the bow, the square sail swelling out from the bamboo mast like the breast of a proud peacock. This trim craft was narrow enough to slip into the twisty channels that crisscrossed the delta where the Hooghly and the Ganges rivers flowed, and this was an advantage when soldiers or angry merchants went in hot pursuit. Yet the dinghy was sturdy enough to brave the ocean, at least in the ordinarily quiet waters where the mouth of the Ganges emptied into the

Bay of Bengal. Still, the men rarely took Jamini out into the open sea unless a storm had just passed by, for it was then that the ocean might yield up treasure from the cargo of a wreck.

The boy was too small to work the oars or the oversized paddle at the stern that steered the boat, but his eyes were as sharp as youth could make them, and it was his task to serve as lookout for the small band manning the boat. He should have been looking for salvage, but half the time he found himself keeping his eyes on the members of the crew. He could see four of them, but the one who worried him was the fifth, the one called Girish, who was hidden, very likely asleep, in the small cabin of matting and bamboo. Girish was their leader, and Girish frightened him. The beatings didn't matter; the boy expected as much. One night not long ago, however, when purses were full and hashish smoke turned the air into perfume, Girish had done something strange. He approached Jamini with a smile and a hug, then drew the boy away from the other men with the promise of a secret to be shared; but the secret was not a pleasant one, and the boy had run away from his naked master.

Since then Jamini had kept out of sight as much as he could, but there was nowhere to hide on such a small boat. He prayed to the gods he had passed in their temples, the gods whose names he hardly knew, to help him find a treasure in the sea, a prize to satisfy the greed of any man, so that they could return before dark to the safety of the shore. He looked to the west and saw only the burning orange of the sinking sun, its glare still half blinding him when he turned to the east and saw something like a shadow dancing on the waves. He squinted, rubbed his eyes, and looked again.

"There!" he shouted. "A box!"

The man at the tiller, whose post at the high stern gave him an advantageous view, peered out over the water and then shrugged. Jamini pointed, shouted again, then scampered up the side of the cabin's curved bamboo frame and took the tiller into his own hands. Almost dancing with excitement, the boy was pushed roughly out of the way, and might have fallen overboard if he had not caught himself in the sail's simple rigging. The slender mast bent, the entire dinghy shuddered, and the men in the bow rested their oars as they turned to watch the boy dangling from the ropes as he cried out to them.

"You're all blind! Can't you see it? A big box!"

The man beside Jamini dropped the rudder and pulled him down from the ropes, but in an instant he was shouting along with the boy. He began to steer toward the east, and his companions worked their narrow paddles with new enthusiasm. The boy was laughing, all fear of Girish banished from his mind, when a hand shot out from the low cabin and clutched at his right ankle. Jamini staggered and slammed down on the rough deck. The back of his head struck the boards first, and patches of light and dark obscured his vision for a moment before they cleared away to show the snarling face of Girish.

"What's this noise, you monkey? Would you wake the dead?" Girish twisted the boy's arm and pulled him upright. The leader was the biggest of his band of scavengers, as well as the fiercest; his black beard was ragged and his long hair almost hid the fact that he had lost an ear. He wore a turban and a loincloth like the others, but he alone among them was draped in a dhoti, a ragged scrap of soiled cloth which was wrapped around his body like a ceremonial garment, lending him a shred of dignity which his behavior hardly justified, especially when he was pummeling a small boy.

"You like to jump, don't you, Jamini? Would you like to hop? You might be more use to us with one leg at that! At least a beggar boy makes some money, which is more than you do!"

Jamini shivered, and not just from the cool breeze that wafted across the water as the sun slipped down into the shadows of the west. He knew all too well how many children in the streets of Calcutta had been maimed or mutilated by their own families so that they would appear more pitiful when they cried out for alms. A crippled boy might support his family while a healthy one starved, and Girish had no blood ties to make him squeamish about what happened to the boy who squirmed in his grasp.

"But I've found something," Jamini stammered. "Something big! Look," he implored, rolling his eyes toward the area where he had spotted his prize. Girish squinted into the dusk and shook his head.

"It's true," said the helmsman. "A box bigger than I am. We'll need the nets to haul it on board."

Girish relaxed his grip for an instant and the boy wriggled away, ducking down into the little cabin which reeked with the sweat of men and the blood of fish. The red light of evening cast a latticework of shadows through the crudely woven matting over his head; he could see the pattern on his hands as he reached for the nets. He pulled them out to the deck where larger hands than his reached down for them, then he ducked back into his shelter, out of sight and hoping to be forgotten. He heard the voice of Girish bellowing orders, and he wondered how much louder that voice would be if the box proved to be empty. Jamini longed for something wonderful, for a god or a demon to rise out of the treasure chest and grant his every wish, but he would have been satisfied with anything Girish could sell, anything that could calm that brutal anger.

21

Still, magic would be best. The boy peeked through the chinks in the cabin at the black silhouettes of men against the sky, casting their nets wide over the ocean as the dinghy turned and swayed against the waves of ebony and jade.

Something hit the side of the boat with a tremendous thump; Jamini felt himself rocked back and forth for a moment as if a storm had struck. "We have it now," Girish called out. "Don't let it get away!"

Jamini slipped from the cabin and hid himself behind it, his head poking out over the top to watch Girish and three of his men bent over the side while the helmsman in the stern held the boat on course. "It's slipping," someone grunted, and the thief named Ajit made a flailing lunge that sent him screaming overboard. Jamini began to laugh, but then the boat rode up again and there was another heavy thump, not quite like the one before. The helmsman looked down and moaned; Girish cursed; Ajit had stopped screaming.

Jamini rushed to the side and looked down. The long black chest, free of the net, was slipping away to the stern as the boat moved forward. At first there was no sign of Ajit, but as the box bobbed on the gently moving water he suddenly emerged beside it, floating languidly in the black water. It was too dark to be sure, but Jamini thought the man's head was the wrong shape.

Only the sea spoke while the corpse drifted quietly away. Then Girish whirled and caught Jamini by the throat. "You see what your box has done? It's killed a man! It crushed him! Better you had never found it, boy, but since you did, you stay with it!"

Jamini felt himself swung up into the air and over the side; before he had time to cry out he dropped with a splash into the sea. He struggled briefly in the icy silence

22

beneath the waves, hardly sure which way was up until the chill of panic sent him gasping to the surface. He whipped his head wildly around and saw the boat rushing away into the night, its sail billowing in the evening breeze. He reached an arm out longingly, but realized at once that he had no chance of catching up. His only hope lay with the sinister black box that floated peacefully a few feet away. If there was a god inside, then it must be a cruel one, for it had already killed a man, but Jamini swam a few strokes and clutched at the wooden sides. He wanted to cry for help, but knew that this would only please Girish, so he stayed silent.

The boy knew that he was miles from land, farther than he could ever hope to swim. The Bay of Bengal was as vast in his eyes as the dark sky arching over him; Calcutta was as distant as the faintly shimmering stars. The dinghy was out of sight and the light of day had almost disappeared as well. In a few minutes he would be swallowed by the night, but the awe he felt in the face of his utter loneliness was almost greater than his fear for his own life. Buoyed up by waves and wood, he felt somehow that he was only dreaming of his death.

A speck of orange fire appeared in front of him. Puzzled, he stared as it was joined by another, the two flames like the eyes of a wild beast. They grew larger and closer, a black shadow bulking up behind them, until Jamini finally saw that they were torches, held aloft by men in a dinghy. Girish had come back for him, or for the box.

"Have you opened it yet, boy?" The harsh voice cut through the night air as the boat drew alongside, and Jamini, perhaps because he had been too long in the water, felt a shiver run through him. He didn't know what answer he was expected to give, but he did know enough to swim away from the black chest as the dinghy approached: he had no desire to be crushed between them now that rescue was at hand.

He saw the nets cast out again and the box snared, caught between reflections from the torches as it bumped and rattled against the boat's side. He watched the men straining to haul their treasure up, the torches swaying as the deck tipped toward the water ominously.

"Stop pulling!" Girish commanded. "It's too heavy. We'll capsize." His gaze fell on Jamini, who was paddling forward in the hope that he at least might be taken on board if his discovery could not. "You!" said Girish. "It's your box. Open it!"

Eyes wide, Jamini stared up at him in disbelief, and without even realizing he began to back away. "Do it," Girish insisted, "or you'll be left here for good." A knife with a curved blade gleamed in his hand, then flashed downward to embed itself in the dark wood. "Use that, and be quick about it!"

Jamini hardly knew if he was more frightened of Girish or of the chest, but he decided in an instant that his only chance for survival lay in doing as he was told. At least that would bring him closer to the dinghy. Cold and wet and still half expecting to die, the boy swam a few strokes forward, reached out for the sinister raft, and grasped at the hilt of the dagger with his right hand. He put the weapon between his teeth, treading water as he felt along the sides of the box. He found hinges but no latch, not even when he shifted the rectangular bulk around so that he could avoid the space between it and the boat's slippery side. The box seemed to be sealed shut. He looked up helplessly.

"Do it or drown," Girish said.

The boy had never had to swim for such a long time in his life. His lips were trembling from the chill and he felt a cramp forming in his leg: without something to cling to, just staying afloat would be impossible for him quite soon. He tried to use the knife, wedging the curved blade into the crack under the lid of the chest, but the space was too narrow to admit more than the tip. He tried to force it with both hands, and to his horror he dropped below the surface of the sea, his fingers clutching desperately. He dragged himself up by the dagger's hilt, sputtering and shaking as he gasped for breath, then fell back as the blade snapped off in his hands.

And the lid flew off the box, knocked into the air as though it had been kicked by an elephant. Jamini lay on the gentle waves, too startled to struggle, while two pale hands reached out of the open chest. Distorted by the flickering torchlight, the figure of a man rose up, grasped Girish by the hair, and pulled him down into the darkness.

Shouts filled the sky. One torch fell in the water; an instant later the other was snuffed out. The boy heard shuffling, a splash, a wail that sounded too high-pitched to have come from a man's throat. Like the others on the boat, Jamini had never seen a coffin, but he knew now that the box had concealed a spirit of great power and that somehow he had set it free. He thought longingly of the wishes he might make, and then he sank again into the sea.

What happened after that he never knew, but when he awoke, he found himself in the dinghy's cabin of matting and bamboo. He recognized it by the smell, and then by the faint red light that shone through the latticework as it had that evening. Had he been dreaming? He slipped out onto the deck and saw a single torch flaming in its socket at the bow. The demon stood beside it, dressed all in black, plying a single oar with the strength of an entire crew. Its eyes were dark hollows, but its sharp teeth were bright as it smiled at him, and its lips were splashed with blood. They were the only ones on board.

The boy felt as if he had been understood completely in the brief moment when their eyes locked, and in the same way he knew what was expected of him without asking. Spirits need no words, and miracles are not to be questioned.

Jamini slipped toward the stern, took the rudder in both hands, and set a course for Calcutta.

# THREE

# The Straw Man

"You'll find your cousin in better spirits tonight, I think."

"You see to it that I do," said Nigel Stone. "I trust there will be no objection if I offer him some food?"

"He's quite well fed, sir, rest assured, but as it's Christmas Eve, there will be no objection as you say."

The change in the man called George had been remarkable. Just a few bank notes had turned him from a menacing brute into a docile old dog whose only motive was to please. Stone was mildly disturbed to realize how little it might cost to put an end to suffering and pain, but more than that he was pleased with the knowledge that his own efforts had made the change possible. He was full of the spirit of the season.

"We still have him under restraint at night," George admitted apologetically. "After all, they say he's a killer. But he's been getting exercise each day, and we've even been giving him something to do with his hands. It seems to calm some of these fellows down, the coconuts.''

"Coconuts?'' echoed Stone, suddenly reminded that he was, after all, in a madhouse.

"We give 'em to the men, just the outsides, you see, and they pluck 'em into pieces. Just the hairy parts.''

Stone stopped in the hallway and turned to look at his guide. "What the devil for?'' he asked.

"It's used to stuff things, like horsehair is. Brings in a bit of money and it keeps the men employed.''

"I can't imagine Reggie Callender doing that,'' said Stone.

"He's much more quiet now,'' the keeper said. "Sometimes it calms 'em down, a few days in the cellar. They realize things could be worse. Take your cousin, sir. He used to be no end of trouble, screaming and fighting, and swearing to get free, but now he seems quite content. Maybe there's something in this reform business, after all.''

"You see to it that he's well taken care of,'' Stone replied, "and you'll be the better for it yourself.''

"Yes, sir. I didn't know, until you came, that we had charge of a gentleman who had a family. This is his room, sir. One of the best.''

The two men stood in the upper floor of Halliwell House, in a corridor which, however bare and bleak, was positively homelike compared to the tunnel hidden beneath the building. And the door they stood before, Stone noted, was the proper size for men to enter standing up. Unconsciously he stamped the remnants of snow from his boots as he prepared to enter.

The keeper put his key into the lock and handed Stone his lantern. "Will you be staying long, sir?''

"Come in ten minutes, if you will. I have a cab waiting for me outside."

The door opened as Stone spoke, and Reginald Callender caught every word Stone uttered. He stiffened, his mind racing, and began to count off the seconds left to him before George would return.

"Hello, Nigel," said Callender.

"Merry Christmas, my dear fellow! Merry Christmas!"

Stone tried to keep the smile on his face as the door closed behind him. After all, he couldn't have expected a luxury suite. This was certainly an improvement, and Reginald Callender looked something like his old self again.

With his beard shaved and his hair trimmed, he might have been a haggard version of the handsome young gentleman of only a few months ago, but his eyes darted wildly from side to side, and his wardrobe was unseemly. His feet were bare, his trousers were of coarse, almost colorless fabric, and above his waist he was wrapped in an ungainly garment with sleeves so long that they were joined together at the back, bound to a long chain that was fastened to a staple in the wall. Still, the room was clean, his clothes were clean, and he was seated in a straight wooden chair which seemed to have been built into a corner of the room. Beneath it, Stone noted with a mixture of shame and relief, there rested a chamber pot. Otherwise the room was empty save for a bed of straw covered with a rough blanket.

"You see what your money can buy," said Callender. "But don't think I'm ungrateful, please. You've seen where I was, and a prisoner can't expect much more than this. They let me walk, sometimes, and they free my hands if I work."

"It's not good enough."

"Only freedom would be good enough, and I can't expect you to provide that."

Stone mumbled in discomfort.

"Never mind." Callender smiled. "You've done more than anyone else would do for me, and I'm quite comfortable here, except that my nose itches abominably."

Stone hurried forward in his snow-spotted black greatcoat, his hat still on his head, then pulled off one of his gloves and obligingly scratched his cousin's nose.

"You may get out one day," he said soothingly, "especially if you'll stop talking about dead men you want to kill again. That just won't do, you know. But if you stay calm and behave yourself, perhaps they'll see that you're not mad at all and let you go."

"You talk as if they sent doctors around each day to observe me. I haven't seen a doctor since my trial. And even if they did decide that I'd gone sane again, what makes you think they wouldn't take me out and hang me? And will you for God's sake stop scratching my nose?"

Stone backed up clumsily and tried to look stern. "That's just the sort of thing I mean," he said. "I only wanted to help you. It looks bad when you lose your temper that way."

"Why shouldn't I lose my temper?" his cousin demanded. "I've lost everything else. I've lost my freedom, I've lost my inheritance, and I've lost the woman I loved."

"Well, you didn't exactly lose her, did you, old fellow? I mean to say, you killed her."

"Newcastle tricked me. I meant to kill him, not her. And I'll kill him yet, whoever he is, however far I have to go. He destroyed me, and I'll destroy him."

"You mustn't talk that way, I say. Especially at Christmas. I can't stay long, but look what I've brought you."

Callender froze. He realized he had actually lost con-

30

trol, and now he had no idea how much time had passed. "You have to leave soon, do you?"

"In a few minutes. I'm off to see a man about a necklace, a gift for my good wife. And I don't think she'd understand if she knew I'd been here."

"Of course," said Callender. He tried to look pathetic, and in fact not much effort was involved.

"But look what I've brought you," chortled Stone. "I feel quite like Father Christmas himself!" He reached deep into one of his coat pockets and pulled out something shapeless that had been carelessly wrapped in brown paper.

"A pork pie," Stone announced, opening the package as he spoke. "Oh. Sorry. This is a cherry tart. But I've got the pork pie somewhere. And an orange too. They're hard to get this time of year, you know."

All at once Stone's hands were full of food. He looked around the tiny room in some bewilderment, hardly knowing where to put the things, and of course Callender made no effort to assist him. Instead he was staring at the door and wondering how much time he had left.

"Here, make a lap, will you?" said Stone. "There. You look just like a boy having a late night feast at school. And wait till you see what else I've got for you! A bottle of the best sherry! I thought that would make you sit up and take notice!"

It was true that Callender had turned abruptly at these last words, his eyes wide and his mouth half open. He gazed enraptured at the thick green glass as Stone pulled the bottle from his coat. "That's good of you, cousin," he said, his ears cocked for any sound from the corridor outside.

"I pulled the cork before I left so we'd have no trouble with it here," Stone said complacently. He opened the

31

bottle and approached his cousin. "This may be a little awkward," he observed.

Callender did all he could to fulfill that prediction. While Stone tried to feed him as if he were a baby, he shook his head and twisted his lips so that most of the mouthful of fine old sherry spilled down his chin; then he went into a spasm of coughing that was only half sham.

"Damn!" said Stone. "I thought you'd have your hands free. You did last time, you know."

"This just won't do," Callender gasped. "I'd like to eat the pie and drink the wine tonight, and save the rest until tomorrow, but I need my hands. You must help me, Nigel."

"But my dear fellow, what can I do?"

"The straitjacket. It isn't locked. There's just a row of hooks there at the back. You can undo them easily."

Stone gave this new idea a moment's thought. "It doesn't seem quite right somehow," he said. "Might mean trouble for both of us."

Callender's mind screamed, but his face still smiled. "Look here," he argued with the voice of sweet reason, "this is torture. You bring me all this and now you won't let me eat. Just unhook it for a minute, will you? There's no window and the door is locked. I surely can't escape. And after all, it's Christmas Eve . . . ."

"Oh, very well," said Stone with rough good nature, "but just for a minute."

Callender's heart felt like it might punch its way out of his chest when he felt his cousin fumbling at his back. Everything seemed to be taking so long. He tried not to squirm, although his only impulse was to look behind him. "You've got your gloves off, don't you?" he finally said.

"I do now," came the cheerful reply. Callender bit his lip.

32

"Here it comes, old man. Just another few seconds . . . there!" Callender felt his arms come free, and it took all his strength to sit still for just a little longer. Were there footsteps sounding in the hall, or was that just blood pounding in his ears?

"That does feel better," he said quietly as he began to work his way out of the jacket. The wine was on the floor between his feet. "Just hide the orange and the tart in the straw over there, will you, cousin? I'll save them for Christmas Day . . ."

Nigel Stone obligingly bent over the rude bed while Callender shrugged off the heavy canvas and reached down for the wine bottle. There wasn't even time to take a drink.

He smashed the heavy green glass over his cousin's head.

Stone gave a grunt that sounded like no more than the exertion of a heavy man bending down, then flopped on the straw and lay quite still. Callender hoped he wasn't dead; he'd find out later when he'd had a chance to switch their clothes. For now, there was only time for the coat and hat.

Even partially undressing a man who didn't move was almost as difficult as escaping from a straitjacket, and Callender was wild with anxiety as he tugged at the heavy sleeves. He felt Stone's breath on his face and answered it with a small sigh. After all, he'd had to hit the man, who would otherwise surely have been charged with aiding an escape. "It's for your own good," Callender muttered as the coat came free.

He slipped into it and clapped the topper on his head, then positioned himself with his back to the door, blocking enough of the entrance that not much but his body would be visible at once to anyone who might come through.

Of course he knew who it would be.

Callender waited in his little prison, ears straining for the slightest sound that might come from outside, and swore that he would never be confined again. He knew that it would only be a moment before the gigantic brute called George arrived, the last important obstacle to his inevitable escape. There was even a cab ready for him outside.

Callender waited.

His hands began to tremble. Surely too much time had already passed? What if the keeper never arrived at all? A thousand things might have detained him; perhaps there was trouble down below. More likely, though, it was a trick of the hulking George, who had shown himself to be a monster far too often for Callender to be deceived by his current disguise.

Callender had a frightful thought. What if he remained here all night with Nigel Stone for company? What would he do when his cousin awoke? The bottle was already broken and he had no other weapon. Should he beat him with the orange? Smash his head against the wall? Would there be any way to keep him quiet without killing him?

"Just keep still, Nigel," Callender whispered. "Rest."

And of course it was at that very moment that Stone chose to moan and stir.

Callender was in a frenzy, afraid to act and afraid not to. He took a hesitant step toward the man sprawled in the straw, then froze at the sound from the corridor. It was George.

The man was actually whistling. The tune had the air of some off-key, unidentifiable carol. Callender felt himself sweating in his cousin's heavy coat. The hat, which was too large, slipped down an inch over his damp fore-

34

head. He heard the rattle of the keys and held his breath. The latch clicked.

"Merry Christmas, George," said Callender.

He turned on his heel, the broken bottle in his hand, and dragged it across his keeper's naked throat. The man was too startled to stop whistling at once, and a gout of blood shot from his puckered lips. His bland expression changed in an instant to puzzlement and then to rage. His huge hands clutched Callender's face in a death grip.

The pain was instantaneous as well as indescribable. Callender was sure the flesh would be ripped from his skull. He tried to twist away and shrieked in agony. Thick fingers thrust their way into his mouth.

He might have been badly injured except for the orange. It had rolled out into the middle of the room, where Callender in his struggles stepped on it, crushed it to a juicy pulp, and slid forward on its skin. He was thrown off his feet, and George was toppled down on top of him.

Callender lay on his back, the breath knocked from his body, while blood gushed over him like wine from a bottle. He was soaked in the stuff before his keeper died.

Crawling out from the dead weight was nasty work, and no sooner was he free than he spied Stone, sitting up in the corner with his head held in his hands. Callender was so furious at this intrusion that he leaped across the room and punched his cousin three times in the face, hurting his right hand more than he would have thought possible.

His hand throbbing and his face raw, Callender cursed his enemies and set about stripping the unconscious form of his cousin.

The boots were too large for him; in fact, everything was too large for him, but that was to be expected. The only thing whose size he hadn't anticipated was Stone's purse. A trip to a jeweler had been mentioned, but still he

35

was astonished to discover that he had just come into almost two hundred pounds. A year ago Callender might have lost that much at cards without a second thought, but nonetheless it was a small fortune, enough to keep a modest man afloat for years.

He trussed Stone up in the straitjacket, and gagged him with the trousers the asylum had provided. It was some consolation to Callender (as it would doubtless be to Stone) to reflect that the garment was relatively clean. Of course his cousin was ill dressed below the waist, which might prove chilly as well as shameful, but Callender had done all he could.

His last consideration was the straw bed on the floor. It was partly soaked in the widening puddle of George's blood, but there was enough straw still untouched to serve his purpose. He pulled it out by the handful and stuffed it into his oversized clothing. With its aid, his gaunt frame might be full enough to let him pass for even as stout a man as Nigel Stone.

The straw itched intolerably even where it fitted best; at its worst, it felt like a thousand needles digging into his naked flesh. He might even have been happier stuffing himself with the husks of coconuts, Callender thought, but those had all been sold. Finally he felt full enough, and he pulled on his cousin's blood-soaked greatcoat. The blood might draw attention, but he counted on the darkness to disguise him. A man out on Christmas Eve without a coat might be even more conspicuous.

Callender plucked up the keys that George had dropped. They were sticky with gore, and he could only hope they would function in that state. He had nothing to clean them, any more than he had anything to clean the coat. And he had to hurry. He took one last look around, and was riveted by the outraged gaze of his recovered cousin's eyes.

He wanted to say something, be it cruel or kind, but words failed him. He went out through the door and locked it.

The hall was empty. Tempted to skulk in the shadows, he was nonetheless aware that his safety lay in acting as though he were entitled to walk free. He strode down the corridor toward the stairs, wishing he could find a way to imitate Stone's behavior more perfectly. Still, everything he knew led him to believe that there should be no other keepers in Halliwell House tonight.

For an instant, he toyed with the idea of releasing all the other prisoners; he had the keys in his hand. What could be more wonderful than to unleash dozens of maniacs upon the world? Not only that, but they might muddle the details of his own escape. Tempting though it was, Callender decided against the idea. He might unleash something he could not control; he might even risk injury to himself. He had seen again tonight that there were no limits to human cruelty: George had tried to kill him, and his own cousin had tried to hurt his fists with his face. Callender would escape alone.

He slipped down the stairs, walking with unnatural caution despite all his theories that he should behave like an innocent man, and encountered his first locked door at what he suspected was the entrance to the keeper's inner sanctum. Hours seemed to pass before he found the proper key, and when he finally gained entrance, he all but ran across the floor, only to be stopped at once by the double door that led to freedom. Momentarily stymied by another locksmith's problem, he glanced anxiously around the room and spotted the keeper's nightly portion of gin. He took a swig to calm his nerves, then decided to take the bottle with him. As an afterthought, he picked up the poker from the fireplace as well. A weapon was never out of place, especially since he still had to pass the guard at the gate. He thought the straw in his clothing would drive him mad.

He got through the double doors, down the hallway, and out the entrance of Halliwell House before he stopped. The icy air of freedom was more intoxicating than the gin. After months of imprisonment, the sight of the open sky made his head swim. A few flakes of snow fell on his upturned face. He wanted to cry out with delight, but there was still a wall between him and the street.

As he walked briskly toward the little man at the gate, straw digging into him with every step, Callender's hand gripped the poker hidden in his coat. His impersonation might not be successful, after all, and he was not about to be thwarted within ten feet of his cousin's cab. Approaching the dead tree by the wall, he realized with a mixture of horror and delight that the guard was fast asleep on his stool. Callender was stuffed with straw, his hat was pulled low, and his collar was turned up, but the disguise might not be completely effective, and a blow from the poker most certainly would. Should he risk waking the man, or risk putting him to sleep forever?

The poker was half out of Callender's coat when he stepped on a broken branch that snapped like a gunshot. Sufficiently startled and guilty to hide the poker in a flash, Callender saw the guard spring to life and knew that he would have to depend on the straw. A struggle might bring a shout, and there was a witness waiting on the far side of the wall. Callender endeavored to concoct a method to distract the man and found the answer in his cousin's purse.

"Going out now, sir?"

Callender answered with a grunt, his face averted, and held out a small gold coin. The guard took the bait with all best wishes for the holiday season and opened the last barrier as if he feared the unexpected bounty might be snatched away. Callender stepped out into London.

He hurried toward the cab, the most beautiful conveyance he had ever seen. He almost threw his arms around the tired old horse's neck. "Limehouse," he whispered to the driver. "The docks. And be quick about it."

"Look here! That's not what you told me . . ."

"Never mind what I told you. Just do as I say now and you'll be well paid for it. You'll have as fine a goose as any man in London!"

The whip cracked, the horse snorted, the wheels turned, and Callender was off in search of a dead man. His purse was full, but he wondered about the advisability of buying a ticket for Calcutta. It might be more prudent to work his way across, saving the money for what might be a long stay in India. The choice was hardly his, though; he would be obliged to take the first passage that presented itself. The main objective was to be out of England at the earliest opportunity. Then he would be truly free, or as free as he could be until he had destroyed Sebastian Newcastle.

Children in the streets sang of new birth, and Callender grinned and hugged himself as the cab rolled through the night.

Nigel Stone was found on Christmas morning, half naked and trussed up in a straitjacket with only a bloody corpse for company. It took some time for him to explain affairs to the authorities, and he was thoroughly chastised before he was sent home. All in all, it had been the worst Christmas of his life, and in times to come he was content to leave charity to others.

*F O U R*

# *The Dead Man*

The dead man walked through the streets of the city. He arose at dusk, when the sky was red and black bats flew, when jackals roamed among outlying buildings and sullied the night with their ungodly howls. After dark, in the gray fog and the winter wind, the slums by the river might almost have been part of London, but this was Calcutta, nearly five thousand miles away.

Sometimes the dead man walked alone, and sometimes a boy walked with him. The boy had decided that his companion must be a demon from England, for when they sold the boat and took lodgings in the city he gave his name as Sebastian Newcastle. Yet he studiously avoided the center of Calcutta, where the English had been erecting their great temples to commerce and to government for well over a century, insisting instead on wandering through the district to the north, where people from all over India had settled in squalor to serve their English masters. And Sebastian Newcastle rarely spoke English; in fact, he rarely spoke at all, but he seemed able to peer into the boy's mind and pull words out of it, so that soon he could communicate in Bengali, the language whose name the boy did not even know. To him, it was simply the way that all sane human beings expressed themselves. Perhaps the demon was only pretending to be English, for with his long black hair and drooping mustache he would have looked more like a Hindu than a foreigner if not for his skin, which was as white as the ivory from an elephant's tusk. He even had a long scar down the left side of his face which made him look like a thief or a murderer. In fact, he would certainly have been a thief if he had not been a demon, for how else could he have acquired so much gold? He never worked, and he seemed to have no property except the box he slept in.

And the first question he asked the boy was: "What do you know of the goddess Kali?"

Jamini knew little enough of any god or goddess, for he had grown up as much as he had without the benefit of religion, but he was quick-witted and eager to please, especially when for the first time in his life he had a roof over his head and enough food to eat. He could even have worn fine clothes if he had liked the way they felt and hadn't minded drawing attention to himself. In short, he would have done anything for Sebastian Newcastle, even if he hadn't been afraid of him.

So the boy cheerfully spent his sunlit hours in search of the goddess called Kali. The task did not seem formidable at first. One bright afternoon he wandered toward the southern part of the city, to the quarter known as Kalighat, where everyone had told him Kali could be found. Munching on the candy made of almond paste which had become his greatest vice, Jamini fell in with a crowd which

41

seemed to grow like a plague of locusts, clogging the streets that led toward the square where the shrine of the goddess stood. Prosperous pilgrims mingled with the most desperate beggars, and Jamini felt just a bit guilty about the candy when he heard children around him pleading for food. Not long ago he had been one of them, but he told himself that he might offend his private demon by sharing his bounty. The boy was even more ashamed of himself when he spotted a sneak thief relieving a plump worshiper of his purse, for Jamini's conscience told him that he should be working too. Yet he had been told to seek and not to steal, so Jamini chose obedience over enterprise.

He could smell the goddess better than he could see her. Incense sweetened the afternoon air, but the mob blocked his view so that he could only catch an occasional glimpse of the temple in the courtyard beyond the railings. He saw steps covered with yellow marigolds and draped with strings of tiny bells; at the top was a bed of green leaves upon which pilgrims were placing choice morsels of food. Jamini told himself that he was here to learn, though, not to worship, and in any case he had already finished his candy.

He heard people make remarks suggesting that only the devout were welcome in the shrine itself, and while Jamini was hardly one to fawn upon tradition, he decided to be discreet after he saw the sacrifice on the stone block in the courtyard. It was only a goat whose life was offered up to Kali, after all, but when its head was chopped off with a dull steel blade Jamini felt a certain sympathy, coupled with a distinct desire not to outstay his welcome. He did dodge through the crowd for long enough to peek at the goddess, but as he suspected she was made of stone. And she had too many arms.

Sebastian Newcastle was not pleased with this report and demanded to be taken to the place himself. He seemed disappointed that no men or women had been slaughtered along with the goat and told the boy stories of another land, in another time, where gods had demanded the lives of youths and maidens not much older than Jamini himself, and gained great powers from the practice. The boy preferred his own time and his own country, but thought it wiser not to mention this.

The shrine of Kali was more sinister by night, a black bulk in a deserted square. The boy watched Sebastian Newcastle circle it with his head raised and his aristocratic nostrils wide; he seemed to be sniffing for something other than incense. "How old is this temple?" he asked.

Jamini did not know.

"Were men ever killed to please the goddess here?"

"Not while I was watching."

The demon put his hand on the boy's shoulder, and Jamini was startled to feel how cold it was. He flinched almost imperceptibly at the touch and at the question that accompanied it: "Is there anyone in Calcutta as ignorant as you?"

"Only you, great demon," the boy replied before he could stop himself. He put his hand to his mouth and began to back away. "Are you going to kill me now?" he asked.

Sebastian Newcastle showed his sharp teeth for a moment, but Jamini could not decide if he had seen a snarl or a smile. "To kill you would be to tear out my own eyes," Sebastian said. "There is much for both of us to learn, and you can see in the sunlight when I cannot. Just remain as ignorant about me as you are about everything else, and you will have nothing to fear from me."

"I am your devoted servant," said the boy. "No one in Calcutta has a nobler master."

"We serve each other, and I will protect you for as long as you are loyal to me. Stay here now and watch for an Englishman."

Jamini puzzled over this enigmatic order, then forgot it entirely when he saw what the demon was doing. His long black hair was dissolving into smoke, his pale flesh glowing till the skull seemed to show beneath it like a shadow. Then there was only smoke and shadow, and a faint luminescence that faded away and became one with the night's sparse fog. The boy was aghast and alone, yet more convinced than ever that some great power protected him. He watched as tendrils of gray mist drifted up the temple steps, and guessed that Sebastian Newcastle was on his way to visit the goddess called Kali.

Jamini imagined that his demon might be lonely with only a stupid boy for company; why else would he be looking for Kali? Yet he was certain to be disappointed, since the goddess inside was only made of stone. How was it that she had so many followers, and such a fine house to live in, while Sebastian lay unnoticed in a shabby room? The injustice of it all gnawed at the boy. He wanted to become a priest, to build a shrine, to lead pilgrims to worship at his master's feet, but he had been sworn to strict secrecy. Surely the ways of the gods were hard.

A sudden noise interrupted the boy's reverie. He was instantly alert, his street urchin's experience drawing him into the deepest shadows while his wide eyes scanned the square for an enemy and an escape. He still looked like a beggar, and he was grateful for that, since it meant that thieves would hardly be inclined to bother him, but he could not help thinking of the wild animals that sometimes stalked through Calcutta. It was unlikely that they would come so far into the city, but that theory carried little enough weight until Jamini noticed the man leaning against a wall at the end of the street. Evidently he was the source of the sound, and now he was having trouble standing up.

Jamini had seen men like this before, and in fact had

robbed more than one of them, but he had been told to stay in one place, and would certainly have obeyed if he had not noticed that the stranger's hair and beard were of that peculiar red color which marked him, even more than his clothing, as an Englishman. No doubt this was the one Sebastian had foreseen. The boy stepped forward cautiously and crossed the square on bare feet that were silent as the grave. He was almost close enough to touch the man before he heard the song he was humming to himself.

The tune seemed to be changing constantly, but Jamini endeavored to follow it with all the concentration he could muster, convinced that this vagrant scrap of music might be somehow transformed into a bond between him and the man with the red beard. He began to hum along, determined to make any effort that might convince the inebriated Englishman to linger in the square until Sebastian returned, but when his companion finally noticed the boy, wide-eyed, nodding, and apparently enraptured, he was so startled that he instantly fell silent. He looked at Jamini, and Jamini looked at him.

"What are you doing here, boy?"

Jamini, who understood not a word of this, smiled and took up the tune again. Each of the pair of chance acquaintances was bewildered by their meeting, but the boy had a purpose, and so he prevailed.

"Want to sing, do you? Then listen to me. You're doing it all wrong."

The Englishman bent down like a patient parent, his hands on his knees, and lined out the melody with a vigor that was more impressive than his voice. Jamini tried earnestly to follow him, and might have learned some dubious terms in a new language if they had not been interrupted.

"Does my servant trouble you?"

Sebastian Newcastle stood beside them. He had approached so silently that he startled even Jamini, but the Englishman merely stood up, staggering slightly, and leaned against the wall behind him while he regarded the tall man in black with half-closed eyes. "He's not much trouble, but he's not much of a singer either. Couldn't you at least teach him to speak English?"

"Perhaps I shall. He is new, you see, as I am new in India. We intend to teach each other."

"Then you should teach him not to take you to a place like this so late at night. This used to be quite a dangerous neighborhood a few years ago."

"Used to be?" Sebastian asked.

"You see that temple there? That belongs to Kali, one of the Hindu goddesses. They all worship her here, I suppose, but some of 'em used to do it by committing murder."

"A strange form of worship, surely?"

"Not really. Once people accept superstition, they're ready to do anything."

"You speak like a man who has no beliefs at all," Sebastian observed.

"That about sums it up: I'm a journalist. Wakefield, of the *Bengal Gazette.*"

"My name is Newcastle, Mr. Wakefield."

Jamini watched the two of them shaking hands and wondered what it meant. His gaze shifted back and forth between the dark demon and the stranger with the fiery beard, whose soiled suit had once been as white as Sebastian's skin. He wished he knew what they were talking about, and when Sebastian might strike.

Wakefield released his grip and peered at Sebastian with eyes that showed intelligence as well as intoxication. "Your hand's uncommonly cold," he said. "You haven't come here for your health, have you? Because this is the filthiest climate in the world. It's not so bad now, in the winter, but you wait a few months. You'll think you're in hell.''

"Perhaps I am already, in a country where men kill to please their gods. What did you say those men were called?''

"Thugs," answered Wakefield, and all at once Jamini's mouth dropped open. He looked around the shadowed square with wild eyes.

"That's one word the boy understands," Wakefield observed. "Of course it's in his own language. These Thugs were the terror of the land for centuries, but the natives never spoke of them, and it wasn't till a few years ago that they were wiped out. First story I covered when I came here.''

"And you say they are all gone now?''

"Thousands were caught or killed. Had to build new jails to hold 'em all. Still, a few must have escaped. Just stands to reason.''

"Yes," Sebastian said. "But clearly this temple is not the place to find them.''

"Just as well for both of us, Newcastle. But it's no place for an Englishman at night.''

"Yet something brought *you* here, I see.''

"I'm drunk," said the man with the red beard. "And I'm looking around the city for the last time. Off for England soon, now that my fortune's made.''

"You have done well for a man in your profession.''

"Nothing to do with it. It's trade that makes the money here. Just keep your eyes open, as I did. Whole country's ripe for the picking.''

"I shall remember that," Sebastian Newcastle said.

His gaze was so strange that it caused Wakefield to recall suddenly that he was conversing with a stranger on an empty street at night, and had even told the man that he had money. A chill invaded him that was something like sobriety, but even less pleasant.

"I must bid you good night now, sir," he said, "you and your servant. I must get ready to sail."

The man with the dark eyes and the scar that now seemed sinister did not reply. Neither did he move to make way for Wakefield. The boy said something that the man with red hair could not interpret.

The blind eye of the moon peeped out from behind its lid of purple cloud, and in its white light the Englishman fled. Sebastian did not move. Jamini stared at the demon and listened to the fading footsteps until they were gone.

"But you were waiting for him," the boy protested. "You knew he would come."

"I only imagined that he might," Sebastian said.

"But why didn't you kill him? It would have been so easy!"

"Perhaps because of that, Jamini. And perhaps because he did me a service. And he was going home."

After that night the two of them sought Kali in other quarters of the city, for Sebastian had agreed with Jamini on one thing at least: the goddess in the shrine was no more than stone.

The boy and the demon he worshiped became students of squalor, spending their evenings in the slums on the outskirts of Calcutta. Few Englishmen would have dared to venture into these sinkholes of poverty and pestilence, and fewer still could have thought of a reason for doing so, but Sebastian Newcastle was looking for murderers.

It became his habit to roam through the worst sections of the city, to all appearances a traveler with no more escort than a small boy whose eyes darted nervously from side to side at every sound. And Jamini was frightened at first, knowing well how little life was valued among desperate men, until experience convinced him that he had nothing to fear from anyone while he walked in Sebastian's shadow.

And in truth most of the people they encountered in their nocturnal pilgrimages were less threatening than pathetic. Calcutta was a city that the British had built where no city had been before, and the hope of employment had lured countless Indians into a life where they really had no hope at all. Far from the paved streets, far from the grandiose structures that housed the empire and the East India Company (as if the two could be separated), the refuse of a nation huddled together in the darkness.

Many simply slept where they found themselves when they could walk no more, beside the roads and beside ditches that could not even be called gutters unless they were improved. The scrawny bodies scattered everywhere were motionless, and only the vultures that flapped down occasionally from the sky could tell the sleeping from the dead. The stronger and more enterprising built fires and camped next to them; the orange flames lit hundreds of corners, and the bitter smoke mingled with the fog of winter.

Few even looked up when the tall man in black clothing passed them by; time had wearied them and hardened them so that they could not even dream that help might be forthcoming from a stranger. Yet sometimes one dared to be bolder, most frequently a beggar whose pleas for assistance had long ago become an unbreakable habit. Jamini took it upon himself to keep these interlopers at bay, driving them off with the practiced callousness of one to whom even the most pitiable deformities were commonplace. When he encountered a boy with a begging bowl in his teeth, and wooden blocks were his hands and feet should have been, Jamini employed unusually energetic shouts and screams to send the apparition clattering away; it reminded him too vividly of what he might have become himself.

Far to the north, where the filthy alleys that ran with sewage began to merge with the marshes and jungles of the delta, where lean-tos made of discarded boards and other refuse gave way to huts of twigs and reeds, Sebastian finally found the men he wanted. They were no ordinary cutthroats, like the ones Jamini had seen his demon slaughter with his hands and then devour. In fact, they spilled no blood at all, and they were only discovered when Sebastian had decided to seek for them no more.

Jamini never counted days or nights, but he had wandered with Sebastian for long enough to see winter giving way to spring, and to see his demon yielding to despair. "They are all dead," Sebastian decided, "and their goddess is dead as well. A force such as she must have been cannot survive without the faith of many worshipers."

"But people are still afraid of Kali," said the boy, "and of the Thugs too."

"Men fear many things that do not exist, Jamini, and it takes more than fear to make them true."

The boy, who had no reply for this, sat down beside his master on a rock that seemed to be growing out of the ground beside a stand of cedar trees. Sebastian's shoulders were bowed, and his black hair hung down and covered his face. Jamini unconsciously mimicked this posture, and the two of them must have looked like a pair of weary travelers, perhaps a father and son who had lost their way, for very shortly they received the greeting that had been reserved for such lonely pilgrims for hundreds of years.

Jamini was about to speak when suddenly he felt the need to cough, and then he couldn't manage that because it was impossible to breathe. Before he had a chance to think, he was yanked over backward, striking his head on the rock as he stared with bulging eyes into the upsidedown face of a bearded man who smiled at him.

The face grew dim before Jamini even thought of struggling, and he would have been dead in an instant if his assailants had not prudently concluded that Sebastian was the more dangerous prey. As a result Jamini's demon was set upon first, and so had time to free himself while there was still breath in the boy. Jamini never knew what happened, but by the time he could see and stand again he was alone with the corpses of two strangers. The sound of screaming came from the nearby woods.

Jamini would have run if not for his faith in his demon, especially after an uncanny quiet settled over the grove of trees. No birds or animals gave vent to their cries; not even an insect hummed. There seemed to be nothing in the world but death and darkness and a small boy. But there was one more thing: a yellow silk scarf draped on his bare shoulders.

Jamini touched the scarf; it was slippery and cold. He shuddered; he knew what it was. The sacred weapon of those who served Kali was called the rumel, and Jamini would have recognized it anywhere by the weight of the silver coin that had been tied into one corner to facilitate the strangler's grip. The boy shivered as he touched the little bit of money that had undoubtedly contributed to the deaths of many men; he would not have taken it even if it had been a ruby, not even if he had been alone in the world without the power and protection of Sebastian. The thing was certainly cursed.

Jamini stood alone for a moment lost in thought. Then he sighed, shook his head in denial of his own shamelessness, and slipped the silver coin into the folds of his turban.

At once something came crashing toward him through

the trees, and Jamini jumped into the air as if he had been shot. Two men came rushing at him, but behind them loomed Sebastian, whose strong hands sent them hurtling forward to their knees so that they seemed to be groveling in adoration at Jamini's feet. The two men looked up at him with wild eyes; they seemed both too exhausted and too afraid to move. Both were clean-shaven, their faces pale against dark clothing. The larger of the two held a small iron pick in his right hand but seemed to have forgotten it was there. Sebastian reached down and took it away from him.

"Which one of you leads these men?" Sebastian asked quietly. There was no reply. "Will you make me ask again?"

The larger one turned his head toward his companion and licked his lips. "You killed him," he told Sebastian. "Back there. Beside the tree."

"No. He is not the kind of general who would lead his men. He is a priest, not a warrior."

At this both men fell silent once again.

"I know you are murderers," Sebastian continued, "and you know what I am. Your leader is the only one who will stay with me. Speak the truth!"

Out of the corner of his eye Jamini saw his demon raise his empty hand, and as if it were a signal the one who had spoken before unleashed a torrent of words; he gave the impression of a man who thought he might not be allowed to finish what he was saying.

"He's the one, not me. It's Kalidas Sen there, the silk merchant. He gathered us together again, when we were safe doing nothing, and told us the goddess had chosen him. I was a fool to listen. I was safe, I tell you! But I am not the leader. I am not the one you seek!"

He glanced at his companion nervously and then began

to crawl away from him. At a few yards' distance he stumbled to his feet and began to run. "I am not the one!" he shouted.

Jamini watched as Sebastian raised the small iron pick and hurled it with uncanny accuracy, striking the back of the fleeing Thug's neck. The man staggered as Sebastian leaped after him and Kalidas Sen began to scream.

"Spill no blood! For the love of Kali! No blood!" Jamini clapped his hand over Sen's mouth as he saw Sebastian twist the pick across the dying man's soft throat. A dark fountain gushed forth and Sebastian drank from it as Jamini had seen him do before, never allowing his mouth to touch the wound.

Kalidas Sen groaned and covered his eyes with his fingers, but he made no attempt to resist the boy who held him. When he looked again, it was into the dead white face of Sebastian Newcastle, its eyes dark hollows and its mouth dark with smears of blood.

"Kali will not be angry," Sebastian said, "for she is the goddess of death, and I have come from the dead to be with you. Together we shall give her new life, you and I."

"We must never spill blood," intoned Kalidas Sen. "We slay only with the scarf. And with the sacred pick we hide our sacrifices to Kali."

"We have much to learn from each other, Kalidas Sen. First, you will learn humility. You say the pick is used to bury the dead. Good. Now you will show me. There are dead men hereabouts who must be concealed. Show the boy how this is done. His name is Jamini. And be quick about your work, master of Thugs, for this must be accomplished before dawn. Then you will show us where you live."

*F I V E*

# *The Stoker*

On a stifling morning toward the end of May, Lieutenant Christopher Hawke of the 5th Fusiliers stirred lazily in his quarters at the Dum Dum arsenal on the outskirts of Calcutta. The vestiges of Hawke's military training were still sufficient to rouse him at the sound of a bugle call, however lethargically it had been delivered, but the woman beside him slept on undisturbed. He regarded her with mild distaste. Waking up in India was bad enough; waking up after a night of gin and brandy was even worse; and waking up with a whore in his own bedroom could be cause for a reprimand.

At least she was one of the regimental whores, housed here at Dum Dum to control the spread of disease, so there wasn't much chance that he had caught anything, and he silently thanked the East India Company for that. But she wasn't a white woman, and he didn't even know her name. He pushed her shoulder, not gently, and got only a grunt from her for his trouble. Hawke sighed and sat up with his legs over the edge of the bed and his head hanging forward into the mosquito netting that was draped around him and his companion. He stood up, glanced at the motionless fan above him, and cursed under his breath. Then he kicked the woman's backside with his bare foot. She tumbled out of bed onto the floor, looked up at him sleepily, and smiled mechanically when she realized where she was. Then she saw the expression on his face, and at the sight of that she gathered up her clothes and scurried from the room.

Hawke pulled on his trousers and roared for his tea. At once a young native rushed in carrying an earthenware jug, from which he poured steaming liquid into a cup that was ready on the table near the bed. Hawke could feel the heat radiating from the tea as he brought the cup to his mouth. The sun had only been up for a few minutes, and he was sweating already. It was intolerable.

"Bath!" he shouted, pulling his trousers off again. The tea bearer hurried out and was replaced in less than a minute by two body servants with red clay jars that had been cooling by the windward wall of the bungalow. They followed Hawke out of his bedroom and into a small chamber with a brick floor, and there they dumped gallons of tepid water over their master while he snorted and sputtered and stamped his feet over the drain in the bricks. Towels were ready as soon as he reached for them, and his uniform was laid out in the next room before he stepped through the door. Brown hands buttoned his tunic and pulled on his polished boots; Hawke had nothing to do but stare up at the ceiling once again.

By the time his dressers had stepped back to admire their handiwork, Hawke had worked himself into a rage. He pointed upward. "What's that?" he demanded.

The gaze of the servants followed the direction of his

finger and rested on a contraption of canvas and wood that hung down from the ceiling. "Punkah," one of them said.

"That's right," said Hawke. "It's the damn punkah. And it's not moving, is it?"

"No, sahib."

"Speak English, damn you. Call me 'sir.' And do you know why it's not moving? Because there's no one working this cord, is there?"

Hawke yanked at a piece of heavy string that ran from the fan and down through a hole in the wall. "There should be a punkah boy outside with this tied to his toe, and he should keep that toe moving, but there hasn't been a breath of air in here all night. Is he trying to suffocate me? Bring the punkah boy to me at once!"

The two men bowed and turned, only a step ahead of Hawke as he strode into his sitting room. "And get the boy in here to clean up!" he shouted after them. "And get the bhisti to fetch more water from the well! My God, must I do everything myself?"

He was alone, and suddenly wondering about the tone of his voice. He was a tenor, he supposed, not the best sort of range for a man who wanted to command, and although he had made repeated efforts to speak in a lower register, his fits of temper inevitably brought forth a high thin sound that even he realized was little better than a squeal. It was just one more reason to hate the Hindus.

Hawke sought reassurance in the mirror on his sitting room wall. Surely the waxed spikes of his blond mustache were properly military. Those cold blue eyes exuded authority, no doubt of it, and the monocle, although a man with his vision didn't need it, added a note of dignity. All in all, thought Hawke, he was quite a handsome fellow and a credit to his regiment. The only thing that troubled him was his touch of sunburn. He would have to spend more time in the shade, even if it meant letting a boy follow him around with an umbrella. He simply couldn't allow himself to look like an Indian.

A shuffling sound behind Hawke made him whirl. The punkah boy had come in, his eyes still puffy with sleep, his knees shaking. "Please, sahib," he began, thus immediately striking the wrong note.

"It's too late for all that now," said Hawke in what he hoped was a gruff bass. "You've been sleeping on the job, haven't you? And you want the money you're paid, so you didn't run away. Bring my gloves."

"Gloves, sahib? Sir?"

"Gloves!" snapped Hawke, waving his hands in the air by way of demonstration. "You know what gloves are, and you know why I want them, don't you? It's because I'm going to have to bash you now, and I don't want to dirty my hands on a filthy little wog like you, that's why! Now, bring them at once!"

The punkah boy lowered his head and disappeared into the bedroom, returning a moment later with a pair of white kid gloves which he held at arm's length as if they might be dangerous. Lieutenant Hawke rolled his eyes and groaned. Was there to be no end to his suffering?

"Not like that!" he squealed. "Don't bring them like that, you damned ignorant nigger! Bring them on a tray!"

By noon Hawke was through with the short morning parade and back in his sitting room, half sick from his heavy breakfast of curry and beef chops. Sometimes he thought he should follow the example of the few old hands among his fellow officers and start the day with nothing except fruit, but a man had to keep up his strength, and in any case the native fruit was nasty stuff: the mangoes tasted like turpentine, and the bananas like something that had begun to spoil. Hawke cast aside his copy of the *Bengal Gazette,* which was spotted with his own perspiration and so damp in any case that it was nearly impossible to turn the pages. The temperature had already reached 110 degrees and was still rising; unless there was an emergency, no white man in Calcutta would be expected to do anything more than endure the heat and humidity until sunset. Yet Hawke almost longed for such a crisis, for anything to break the monotony of these endless days, while at the same time he suspected that even the slightest exertion might be the death of him. Surely Calcutta had the most horrible climate in the world. How did the Indians stand it?

He stared up at the punkah above him, now languidly stirring the overheated air into little gusts that were like blasts from an open furnace, and he dared it to stop moving for even an instant. Sprawled in an oversized wicker chair which had arms extended so far that he could prop his feet up on them, Hawke tried to decide which he loathed more: the torrid heat of the spring or the drenching downpours of the monsoon season that would follow. Either way, it would be months before Calcutta was fit for human habitation.

He glanced around the room in a lazy search for some form of distraction, ignoring the brandy and the soda-water bottles that sat on a nearby table. By now half the regiment had undoubtedly embarked on a campaign to stupefy itself with alcohol, but Hawke had promised himself that he would not yield to such temptations, at least not so early in the day, for he was determined to better himself during the ten years which constituted the minimum term of service in India, and he still had eight to go. His books did not tempt him either, least of all the Bengali dictionary which he had once sworn to study, and the cards were not much use without the company of a group of men who had long ago bored him into insensibility. The string of the little banjo he had brought with him from home had long since rotted and rusted, and just the thought of writing a letter to his parents filled him with utter exhaustion. Besides, he had nothing to tell them except that at the age of twenty-four their son was about to go mad from sunstroke and tedium.

A cockroach the size of a small rat scuttled across the floor. Hawke was tempted to crush the disgusting thing, but the stinking liquid mess that would result from such an act of violence was not much of an inducement, and he contented himself with the hope that his visitor would soon depart for a more stimulating environment.

The fan stopped. Hawke contemplated it in something close to a state of shock, then pushed himself up from his chair. This was perhaps the only stimulus that could have made him move. He stumbled out onto the veranda of his bungalow of whitewashed brick and turned, half blinded by the sun, around the corner to where the punkah boy should be. The servant was there, but he was not alone.

"This gentleman for you, sir," said the punkah boy.

Hawke squinted into the white glare of day at the ragged silhouette before him. Whoever it might be, he hardly looked like a gentleman, but at least he was English, a rangy fellow with sandy hair, a shaggy beard, and a floppy straw hat which looked like the product of a native bazaar. His cheap cotton trousers and open shirt were white. Hawke was not impressed, but realized that he himself, barefoot and shirtless, hardly cut a more distinguished figure.

"You'd better come inside," he told the stranger. "And you," he added to his servant, "keep that punkah going if you know what's good for you.

59

"The servants are hopeless," Hawke observed genially as he escorted his visitor into the sitting room, "but at least they're cheap enough."

"And that one does nothing but work that string with his toe?" asked Hawke's visitor.

"Running that fan. About all he's good for, really. None of them can do much of anything, and even if they could, they say their gods won't let them. I've got eight servants myself, and I don't know an officer here with less than half a dozen. Of course in the field we need more . . ."

Hawke trailed off as he noticed that the man with the beard was crouching near the floor, intently examining the hole in the wall that admitted the punkah cord. "I don't like things like this," he muttered, "things that go through walls."

Lieutenant Hawke just stared at him for a few seconds before thinking of something to say: "You're here with the Company, are you?"

"I'm not a soldier," said Hawke's visitor as he stood.

"No, of course not. You'd be wearing a uniform. I meant the East India Company."

"I am here on my own behalf."

"Really?" Hawke polished his monocle with a shirt he had tossed aside and looked at the stranger more carefully. "I don't think I know a white man in Calcutta who isn't with the Company. Why, even the Army works for them. Oh, I suppose there must be a few of Her Majesty's troops about somewhere as well, but the Company runs India, and you won't get much done unless you're in with them. Come to seek your fortune, have you?"

"I have already lost my fortune," said the stranger as he ran a finger over Hawke's chessboard. "What I seek is a man."

"See here!" sputtered Hawke. "Who are you?"

"Don't worry, Hawke, I haven't come for you. You don't recognize me, do you?"

"No. Should I?"

"I suppose not. You don't see me at my best. But you're different too. We were at Eton together."

"No! Really?"

"And you may be the only man on this accursed continent I can trust."

"Sounds a bit melodramatic, don't you think? You'd better tell me your name before you tell me anything more."

"Callender. Reginald Callender."

"Good Lord! Are you sure? I mean of course you are, but you don't look . . . Have a seat, my dear old fellow."

Callender sank into a rickety wooden chair and leaned forward with his arms resting on the table in front of him. "You were going to say that I looked like a common workman, weren't you, Hawke? And that's what I have been. A stoker. I worked my way to India in the engine room of a steamship, shoveling coal into a boiler. Weeks of filth, and sweat, and fire. It was like being in hell."

"Sounds rather like Calcutta," Hawke observed.

Callender sat with his head in his hands, his eyes fixed on the brandy bottle before him as if he could observe the past or future in its depths, but Hawke saw only what was on the table and offered his guest a drink.

"No," said Callender. "I drank enough in London to ruin me, and it would have, too, but I was ruined already."

"What happened?" asked Hawke as he sat down opposite the man who had been the friend of his school days. "I used to envy you sometimes, you know. I thought you had everything a man could wish for."

"I thought so too."

61

"But you had a rich old uncle! And the last I heard a young lady with even more money was engaged to marry you."

"My uncle's money was gone before he died, and then the girl died too. She was killed. Murdered. And I was blamed for it."

"You mean you were in prison?"

"I was in a madhouse. For months."

Hawke had no appropriate response to this remark, only an involuntary image of the bearded man trussed up in a straitjacket and screaming at the top of his lungs. There was a hoarseness in Callender's voice that had never been there before, a quality Hawke had noticed in sergeants who spent their lives shouting at recruits. Had Callender screamed until he damaged his throat? Was he insane?

The only sound in the room came from the slow motion of the fan overhead. Hawke reached for his snuffbox and took a small pinch in each nostril. "You were innocent, of course," he finally said.

"I swear I never meant to hurt her," Callender replied. "It was a mistake. I was tricked into it by the man I'm looking for. He's the one I meant to kill, and when I find him I'll do it. No one believed me, and that's why they put me in that place. He probably thought they'd hang me, but they didn't, and I got away from them, and I came halfway round the world to make him pay for what he did to me. He's got to pay, and you've got to help me."

Callender was becoming agitated, his hands gripping the edge of the table and pushing against it to emphasize his words. Hawke, by contrast, was lounging back in his wicker chair, his eyes half closed. He had longed for a distraction, but not necessarily one like this. Still, the situation might provide at least a bit of entertainment, and if Callender proved to be uncontrollable, he could always be arrested again. Hawke tried to recall what it was that he had liked about the fellow, and couldn't think of much except the money that was now only a memory.

"I suppose this man you want has a name," Hawke said.

"I don't know. He called himself Sebastian Newcastle, but he might have changed that more than once. I think he was some sort of foreigner."

"Well, you know what he looks like, anyway . . ."

"He was very tall," said Callender, closing his eyes to call up an image in his mind, "with long dark hair and a dark mustache."

"A barber could change that as quickly as a man could change his name, you know."

"And he has a scar down the left side of his face. Like a white streak of lightning."

"That's something that can't be altered. Anything else?"

"He's very pale. Pale as a ghost."

"No man stays pale in India."

"This one will. He never goes out in the sun."

"Very sensible, I'm sure. So we have a tall man with a scar who never goes out, and you think he might be somewhere in the city. That shouldn't present much of a problem."

"You really think so?" Callender sat up suddenly.

"No," said Hawke, "but I'm beginning to think you may be mad, after all, old chum. Calcutta is teeming. It's like looking for a tall man in London."

Callender jerked spasmodically, as if he had leaped out of his chair and taken his seat again in the space of a second. "I'm not mad, you know," he said carefully, "and I will find him."

"No doubt, no doubt." Hawke covered his brief flurry

of alarm with an elaborate yawn. He glanced casually around the sitting room, reassuring himself as to the placement of his musket, his sword, and his hog spears. "But you won't get much help from me if that's all the information you have. I'm no magician, Callender."

"Magician," echoed Callender. "But that's what he is. That's why he's here, you see. And don't look at me like that, I tell you I'm all right. You see, this Newcastle made his money as a kind of charlatan, a confidence trickster. He convinced people that he could talk to spirits, call up the dead, that sort of thing. And I believe he came to India to, well, pick up some tricks of the trade, so to speak."

"You mean like the Indian rope trick?"

"Not exactly, no."

"Good. Because there's no such thing. It's just a legend, nothing more. But there are some strange things in India, I'll grant you that."

"I heard some stories about a goddess and the men who worship her," said Callender. "A death cult. Blood sacrifices. That sort of business."

"And you think your man Newcastle is looking for them?"

"I'm banking on it."

"Then I'm afraid both of you are out of luck. There was a bunch like that, years ago, but they were all wiped out. Thousands of 'em jailed or hanged. Thugs, that's what they were called."

"Yes," said Callender excitedly. "Thugs!"

"Your man would have to be a real magician to find a Thug in India today, my dear fellow. Every soldier, every native chief and prince, every man in the country was sworn to put an end to Thuggee. It's gone like yesterday."

"But I tell you it isn't. It can't be! He wouldn't have

come all this way unless he knew. Have any dead bodies been turning up here recently?''

"Dead wogs? More than you can count. They starve in the streets, or drop from one of their foul diseases. A fair share of murders too. But no ritual stranglings with silk scarves, not that I've heard about.''

"I meant something else, Hawke. I meant bodies of people who were bled to death.''

"What?''

"That was Newcastle's method, you see. He took the blood for some foul ceremony he conducted. You see, he got to where he believed in his own powers after a while. He was quite mad, but when I tried to tell Scotland Yard about it, I was the one who got locked up. But you believe me, don't you, Hawke? We were at school together! I took a beating for you, didn't I?''

"Yes, I suppose you did,'' admitted Hawke. "You wouldn't carry tales, not even if it cost you some of your own skin. You were a stubborn lad, I'll give you that.''

"And I'm no weakling, not after what I've been through. A stoker gets strong, you know. And I've got money. All I earned, and more that I got from my cousin when I escaped. We'll work together. What do you say?''

Hawke sat up and leaned forward toward the brandy bottle. "I'm not sure I believe you, Reginald my boy, but you interest me strangely. Finding a new nest of Thugs would be quite something. Sleeman, the man who rounded up the last bunch, ended up a colonel as near as I recall. And they were sly enough so we were here for years before anyone suspected there even was such a thing as Thuggee.''

"Then you will help?'' asked Callender.

Hawke poured himself a drink and examined his companion critically. "Have you got a place to stay?" he asked.

Callender nodded.

"Then be back here tomorrow at noon. This will take some looking into. There's probably nothing to it, but I do know that these people are capable of anything, and they don't like giving up their little games. Old Bentinck, when he was governor-general, swore he'd wiped out Thuggee, but there's another quaint native custom he thought he'd abolished, and it still crops up again from time to time. In fact, we've been informed that something's set for tomorrow, and I've got the job of stopping it. Won't be much of a show, but you might as well come along. Nothing to do with your man Newcastle, of course, even if he is in Calcutta, but it might do you some good to see what these people are like. They're not human, you know."

"Something to do with Thugs?" demanded Callender.

"No, but it does have something to do with what you said before. What you might call a human sacrifice." Hawke tossed back his brandy and examined his companion through a monocle half fogged by heat and perspiration. "Have you ever seen a woman burned alive?"

*S I X*

# *The Silk Merchant*

Kalidas Sen sat cross-legged in front of his shop on Lower Chitpore Road. The early evening sun had turned orange, but it was still hot as a flame, and the silk merchant was grateful for the shadow of the canvas awning embellishing the outside of his establishment. Similarly sheltered, his colleagues up and down the street drifted together in groups of two or three, some of them gathered around a hookah to smoke bhang. All maintained an air of studied indifference to the possibility that a customer might intrude, for this was the fashion in which commerce was conducted in India, but only Kalidas Sen was actually afraid that he might be approached by someone who intended to enter his shop. And unlike the others, the silk merchant sat alone.

The crowds in the street had thinned out as the day faded away, but there were still periods of congestion when life teemed in the narrow passage between rows of windowless buildings, especially since the merchants perched on their straw mats made the pavements all but impassable. More than once Kalidas Sen had experienced an urge to join in the throng and vanish from sight while there was still a chance, yet at the same time he sometimes felt himself trembling with anticipation at the mere thought of the visitor who would be arriving when the sun had set. The silk merchant was thirty-four, but waiting for dark transformed him into the equivalent of a child bride, torn between fear and desire.

A wagon pulled by oxen rumbled past, forcing pedestrians out of its path and leaving a thick cloud of dust in its wake. Kalidas Sen coughed and wished for the rainy season, which would of course cause new troubles but at least would put an end to the heat and dust. He could see only dimly a small figure that appeared to drop from the wagon as it rolled away, but in a moment he recognized the beggar boy, dressed in nothing but turban and loincloth, who served Sebastian Newcastle. The boy was all bright eyes and shining teeth, yet his glee showed something less innocent than the high spirits of youth.

Jamini sauntered up to the shop like a favored customer and gazed insolently down at the silk merchant. Kalidas Sen returned his stare, realized the stupidity of challenging a boy, and lowered his eyes.

"I almost didn't recognize you without your black clothes," the boy said.

"I leave those to your master," muttered the silk merchant, glancing anxiously up and down the street as if afraid to be overheard. Evidently reassured, he nonetheless spoke in a nervous whisper. "He said that he would come at night."

"He will. But he sent me to make sure you would wait for him."

"Of course I will wait."

"He said you might be frightened of him. He said you might try to run away."

"Yes, I am frightened of him. Too frightened to run, boy. What is he?"

"He is my master," answered Jamini proudly.

"And he doesn't scare you?"

"Nothing scares me anymore. He protects me. From pirates, and thieves, and even stranglers."

"Be still!" hissed Kalidas Sen, his hand suddenly clutching at the boy's thin wrist. "Don't ever speak of that."

"He could kill you," said the boy as he disengaged himself from the silk merchant's grip.

"I know. Only yesterday one of my best men died of a fever, and last night your master killed four more. And he says he has come to help me!"

"He can help you if he wants to," Jamini said.

"The goddess must have sent him," Kalidas Sen said to himself.

"What goddess? You mean Kali?"

"You must never mention that name," said Kalidas Sen, just barely resisting the impulse to reach out for the boy again.

"But you have it all backward. The goddess didn't send him. He came here to look for her!"

It suddenly occurred to the boy that he had said more than wisdom might dictate, and the expression on his host's face confirmed that suspicion. Neither of them spoke again for what seemed like a long time; then finally Kalidas Sen broke the silence. "You can't stand here in the street and talk to me like this. It isn't suitable. Any self-respecting shopkeeper would have driven a boy like you away at once."

"He said I must watch you."

"Then watch me from across the way. Already people are looking at us. I can't have people wondering about me."

"But if I stand somewhere else, then they will chase me away instead. Maybe I should buy something. Is there a candy maker in this street?"

"Don't buy anything! You'll only draw attention to yourself. A boy like you shouldn't have money. Does he give you money?"

"All I want. See?" Jamini held out a handful of silver coins and smiled.

"Put that away! Go away, boy! Please."

"I might find some candy in the next street," Jamini suggested.

"That's right. That's a good idea. Do that."

The boy looked doubtful. "He'll kill us both if you're not here when he comes."

"I will be here if only you will leave me alone. Otherwise I will close up my shop and run!"

Jamini gave the matter another instant's thought and then rushed off. Kalidas Sen sighed and turned his gaze inward. He shifted his dhoti, the loose wrapping of white cotton that was his only garment, and when he was more comfortable, he resumed his contemplation of the difficulties that made up the life of a man who had chosen to be a chief among assassins and the high priest to a dreadful deity. It was not the career he had planned for himself.

In fact, the ancient and honorable profession of Thuggee was all but extinct, wiped out by an efficient British Army in the decade between 1826 and 1835. Kalidas Sen had seen his own father hanged, but it was not revenge that had inspired him to revive the half-forgotten rituals of Kali's darker side. His desire was born of need, mated to a hint of magic, and once he beheld the golden goddess his fate was sealed. Perhaps, in fact, his destiny had been determined years before, when as a boy he tasted from his father's hand the sacred goor, the coarse sugar consecrated to Kali, for it was then he had been told that he was now a Thug in spirit, even as if he had consumed the body of the goddess herself. He had been scarcely older than the boy Jamini then, but the memory had lingered within him as surely as the goor, and when he had found the gleaming body of the goddess in its hiding place, he had known what to do. Like thousands of his forebears over untold centuries, he had become a thief and a murderer, consecrating his dark deeds to a divinity that was darker still. He had recruited others who were descended from the cult, and each increase in his wealth and influence had brought with it a greater risk of betrayal and discovery, until at last an unholy apparition had overwhelmed him, its lips smeared with blood like Kali's were. This creature, who seemed scarcely human, might be an avatar of the goddess, heralding her return to earth; or it might be one of those demons, foretold by prophecies from long ago, who would be sent to wreak havoc on a corrupt world. But since the British ruled India with such a heavy hand, might not even the visitation of demons be welcome? The chaos they could cause might serve to set the country free, and had not Kali conquered demons in the ancient days?

The silk merchant brooded on these matters as he sat before his shop, a man alone with much weighing on his mind, so lost in thought that he scarcely noticed when darkness fell. The image that seemed to rise before him was of Kali's golden body, too precious to purloin and too imposing to ignore, but all at once a black shadow loomed over him, banishing all illusion with its undeniable reality.

The shadow spoke his name.

Kalidas Sen shuddered and looked up into the face that had haunted his last night's dreams. The flesh was as pale as the long hair framing it was dark, the eyes as black and fathomless as the starless sky. Black too was the suit Sebastian wore, cut like the clothing of an Englishman, but Kalidas Sen doubted that even England could produce a figure as ominous as this one. A heavy mustache masked the hollow of the mouth, but still he believed that he could see blood in it.

The silk merchant swallowed before he spoke. "You know my name. What shall I call you?"

"In London they called me Sebastian Newcastle."

"But you are not really an Englishman."

"No."

"I will not ask where you have come from. You speak their language well . . ."

"And so do you. It is useful to converse with those who rule, is it not? I have learned only a little of your language from the boy, but if you prefer . . ."

"No. It is best that we both understand each other. The street is empty, and the shops are closed, but still we may be noticed. Will you do me the honor to step inside?"

Sebastian Newcastle nodded his head, and kept it lowered as he followed his host through the low doorway. The space inside was like an oven, the air heavy with incense that covered a stale and sour odor, the walls alive with flies. Kalidas Sen lit a small oil lamp, sat with legs crossed on a cushion, and offered another to his visitor, who knelt on it like a man at prayer.

"I am glad you are not an Englishman, even if you do not know any more about sitting than they do. Look around you and see what the English have done to me."

Even in the faint and flickering light of the small flame, the empty shelves that lined the dank shop were obvious.

Only a few bolts of cloth were visible, and those dusty with neglect.

"Then it is not your other work that has left this shop in such a sorry state?"

The silk merchant was less disturbed by this question than by the abrupt realization that there was not a drop of perspiration on his inquisitor's white face. Whatever it was that had entered his premises, it could not be human.

"This was once a fine establishment. My family owned ships that sailed down the Hooghly and on to China, and back again with the finest silks that anyone has ever seen. But every year they took more, the English and their East India Company. They had money and they owned everything. They raised the taxes on us and they lowered their own prices so that only their goods sold. Every Englishman who comes to Calcutta expects to get rich here, and where do you think the money they get comes from? It comes from men like me!"

"And so you became a thief."

"Not because I must be a thief! I have a golden statue! You will see it, I think, when the time is right. It is not here, you see. I wish I had not told you about it. But I think you know. I think you know very much."

"I know that most men with golden statues would not feel the need to steal, at least not the way you do."

"It is not like money, this statue. I cannot steal from the goddess. She tells me what to do."

"You talk like a patriot, Kalidas Sen, and yet you steal from your countrymen."

"I have no country! The English have stolen it. What can you know of such things? And what do you know of Kali?"

"I wish to know what you know," said Sebastian quietly.

73

"Once this city was hers, and not the English Queen's. It was called Kalikata then, and it was not really a city at all, just swamp and jungle, with a few huts and a small shrine to the goddess because part of her corpse fell to earth there."

The creature called Sebastian Newcastle leaned forward, his head outthrust. Flies were crawling across his face, and even into his eyes, but apparently he did not notice them. "Her corpse?" he asked.

"Yes. After she died (this was very long ago, but the story is true), her husband Siva carried her across the face of the earth, and so great was his grief that the other gods feared he would destroy the world. And so Vishnu, the Preserver, took a great knife and cut the body into little pieces and scattered them everywhere. Kalikata was where one finger fell, and for a long time the faithful worshiped it there, but now there is a great new temple in the city, one that is glorious to behold, but I say the goddess is not in it. I say she is in her house in the jungle, but it is overgrown with vines and only the wild beasts pay homage to her. Kalikata was never meant to be a city. Even the English say men cannot live here, that this land should still be jungle, but it is well placed for trade, and so their people and mine come here and die. Perhaps Kali is happy about that, for she loves death."

"But you said the goddess was no more."

"Because she died?" The silk merchant smiled. "Gods die, but they are born again. So are we all, always, born again. But you understand this, for you have come to pave the way for her, whether you know it or not. You are like her, for you feast on the dead."

"No, Kalidas Sen. It is the living that feed me, and they are only dead when I am done with them. And I am dead myself. But as you say, I have been born again."

74

"Ah. Then you are something like a Vetala, a spirit that lives in a corpse and drains the life out of those it touches."

"I dwell in my own corpse, and what I drain is blood, but life comes with it."

Kalidas Sen should have been more frightened than before of his pale visitor, yet he was not. He felt that he was in the presence of a teacher, a guru sent perhaps by the goddess herself, one who might guide the Thugs but never threaten them. And if some men had fallen who might have served this Newcastle, why it was acknowledged everywhere that the gods were capricious, and that their hungers must be satisfied.

"I see," said Kalidas Sen after a moment. "At first I thought you might be one of the ghouls, but they were never men. I have seen them."

"Tell me about the ghouls."

"But why should I tell what you must surely understand already?"

"To please me. So that I may learn more about you. Tell me a story to pass the time until the boy comes. I am your guest, and it is fitting that you should entertain me."

The silk merchant showed some signs of uneasiness. He shifted on his cushion and brushed flies away. "I am inhospitable," he said. "I should offer you food and drink."

"Not if you wish to remain alive. Tell me about the ghouls."

"I saw them years ago, with my father, when we traveled through the jungle together. He told me what they were and then rushed me away, although he swore to me they would not bother themselves with anyone who lived. They were naked and hairless, and they were feeding on a corpse. I did not like to look at them, but I was only a boy then. It was the night my father first gave me the sugar.''

Kalidas Sen thought he saw a question in his visitor's expression, but the words were not spoken, and after a pause he took up his story once again.

''My father thought the creatures might be special to the goddess, since they ate dead flesh the way she did, but of course she does not do that now, not since one of her first servants looked back and saw her feasting. That was forbidden, and to punish us the great Kali henceforth left our victims where they lay, for us to hide from the eyes of men. But she finally forgave the Thugs and gave us the sacred pick so that we could dig graves. Yet I think she would never forgive us if we spilled blood, and that is why I cried out to you last night.''

''I spill as little as I can,'' Sebastian Newcastle said. ''But it is better if I do not put my teeth into the ones I kill, although my teeth were made for just such work.'' He smiled to show Kalidas Sen just what he meant. ''Still, it is not wise. It can even be dangerous.''

Kalidas Sen stared into the mouth of Sebastian Newcastle and began to speak again, if only to distract himself from what was on display there. ''Of course it is only when we kill for Kali that we must restrain ourselves in the matter of the blood. We can fight. Many of my men have been soldiers. Some served with the British, and others are skilled with the ancient arms of India.''

Sebastian silenced him with a gesture. ''You mean your men use weapons like spears and arrows, weapons made of wood?''

''They kill very well, I promise you!''

''The new ways are better. Teach them to use guns.''

The silk merchant opened his mouth to offer reasonable

opinions about the various techniques for taking human lives.

"There will be no argument," Sebastian insisted. "Those men must learn to use guns. I tell you this just as Kali told you to use the rumel when you kill for her. And why must you use it? Why must you spill no blood?"

"But you know this as well as I do," said Kalidas Sen.

"That will be decided later. Speak!"

"The story says that when the world was young a demon came to destroy mankind, and so great was his size that he could stand on the ocean floor with his head above the waves. Great Kali did battle with him and cut him in twain with her sword, but from each drop of the demon's blood another demon rose, and each of those she killed bled forth many more. And then, as Kali labored, drops of sweat fell from her arms, and these drops became men, and these men were the first Thugs. Kali gave them handkerchiefs and told them how to slay the demons without spilling blood. And ever since, we have used the rumel for the glory of Kali."

"And for your own profit," added Sebastian.

"That is as the goddess wishes."

"Very well. When you kill for Kali, you may use the rumel. But when you fight for me, you will use guns. And as Kali gave you the handkerchiefs, so will I provide you with the proper weapons."

"But who shall we fight?" asked Kalidas Sen.

"Who are your enemies?"

The silk merchant's mouth fell open. "You mean the British. But that is impossible."

Sebastian smiled again. "You do not realize what I am," he said. "Yet you have narrated a parable. Let us reflect on it. Again, why do you kill with the handkerchief?"

77

"Because Kali has commanded it."

"And why will you fight with guns?"

Kalidas Sen stammered, at a loss for words. "I don't know," he finally murmured.

"Because I have commanded it!" Sebastian roared, and all at once he sprang upright, looming over the silk merchant like the statue of an ancient and terrible god. His teeth glittered, and even the dark hollows of his eyes seemed to gleam like silver coins. Kalidas Sen lowered his head, and in another moment he might have been face-down on the earthen floor, but he was distracted by a voice from the door.

It was the boy Jamini. "I knew he would wait for you," he told Sebastian. "He is afraid of you. He is even afraid of me."

The silk merchant arose, half angry and half ashamed, but he said nothing.

"The air is foul in here," observed the boy. "The smoke from that lamp stinks."

"We shall not be here much longer," Sebastian told him. "Have you been fed?"

"I found a man in the next street selling . . ."

"It is enough that you are not hungry. We will be leaving Calcutta tonight. Kalidas Sen has found a new home for us. A proper home, something more befitting us than lodgings in a slum."

Once more the silk merchant was at a loss for words, and once more Sebastian smiled at him. The sight was no more reassuring than before.

"We shall sleep beside the golden goddess," Sebastian said, "where we belong. Where have you hidden her, king of Thugs?"

"I have not hidden her," replied Kalidas Sen. "She has always been there."

"Then she is not yours. And if she is where she has always been, she must be in the old temple, the one you say only the beasts visit. Some of those beasts must be Thugs. And the golden goddess must be hidden, or else the English would have stolen her. Is it not so?"

"She is well hidden," said Kalidas Sen.

"Under the ground, where your men meet to worship her. We shall be happy there. Jamini. You have that little sack of earth I gave you. You have not lost it?"

"I have it with me," said the boy, who had understood little of the conversation until this question was addressed to him in his own language.

Sebastian turned toward his host. "Tomorrow you will find a large box in a lodging house I shall describe to you, and you will have it carried to the temple. Tonight, you will guide us there."

"It is impossible. It is too late. It is too dark."

"Only a few things are impossible, silk merchant. You will show us the way, and we will be transported."

Kalidas Sen was not sure how much of the legend of Kali he believed, but when he and the boy Jamini were borne aloft in the grasp of the great winged monster that had been Sebastian Newcastle, then he most assuredly began to believe in something.

And during his long trek home through the trees and the swamps and the slums, after he had been banished from the ancient shrine by whatever had brought him there, he began to be terribly afraid. He feared for his life, but there was more than that. He feared that such a harbinger of change as this Sebastian Newcastle might in the end make a man like Kalidas Sen seem unimportant to the Thugs, to Kali, and even to himself.

79

## SEVEN

# The Informer

The woman was actually smiling as she walked into the flames. That was the image that Callender could not cast out of his mind. From a distance, as he first saw her, she was only a figure shrouded in a sari of white silk, her head covered and her face averted. Yet even then there was a grace in her movements, and in the flowing lines of her garment, that made her seem almost unearthly, so far was she removed from his memories of Englishwomen with their corsets and crinolines. When she first turned toward him, he was immediately struck with a queasy thrill by the barbarity of a jewel, glistening in the sunlight, which seemed to be embedded in the side of her nose, but then he could see only the flawless golden skin, the broad brow, and the huge dark eyes whose expression was a strange mixture of tranquillity and exaltation.

And it was this look of triumph on the woman's face, as she paced deliberately toward the fire where her husband's corpse was already burning, which heightened the horror Callender felt when he realized that she was about to die and that, even though she was only a Hindu, he was already infatuated with her. So much time had passed since he had been with a woman, or even longed to be, that he suddenly felt like a schoolboy, his face flushed with a heat not to be blamed on the oppressive climate of Calcutta.

Enthralled with the spectacle before him, Callender had completely forgotten that he and Lieutenant Hawke were there to interrupt it, and the first shots fired into the air startled him as much as they did the members of the funeral party on the bank of the river. When the woman stumbled and staggered back from the flames, Callender's first thought was that she had been hit by the musket fire. The pungent scent of gunpowder mingled with the less wholesome smoke from the funeral pyre as he saw her recover her footing and turn her eyes to the grove of trees where Hawke and his men were hidden. The soldiers rushed out and down an incline toward the river while Callender remained lost in his thoughts, his mount stirring restively beneath him. A flick of the reins sent the old horse slowly down the hill, and its rider was still too lost in his reverie to consider the possibility that he was moving into danger.

As it turned out, however, the scene on the bank of the Hooghly looked more like a farce than a tragedy. None of the mourners was armed, and the only resistance offered to the 5th Fusiliers came in the form of shouts and futile attempts to flee. Two of the Hindus leaped into the water as if it were a sanctuary. It was only a branch of the sacred Ganges, Callender reflected, and apparently not endowed with magical properties, for the two men sank like stones and had to be rescued by a pair of laughing and cursing soldiers. The skirmish was over almost before it began,

81

and all sixteen of the Hindus taken into custody. Lieutenant Hawke, instinctively choosing the best role for himself, had trotted up to the woman in white and snatched her from the ground. He took her into his arms without a struggle, and Callender had to admit to himself that the lieutenant, with his red tunic and handsome chestnut stallion, looked very much like a picture-book hero, complete with a damsel in distress. Callender, of course, could only imagine the feel of her warm flesh under the smooth silk.

One of the Hindus, whose black beard matched his turban, began to scream at Hawke, and his tone was less fearful than indignant. Callender did not understand the language, but he was able to infer the import of Hawke's reply, which was accompanied by the slash of a riding crop.

Callender trotted over, drawn by the dark eyes of the Indian woman. She gave him a glance that was impossible to read and then lowered her lids. A fine film of perspiration made her dark face gleam.

"Ah! There you are," said Hawke. "You can see for yourself that some of the old ways do survive, even if they are outlawed. And perhaps the suttee isn't the only bad habit that hasn't been broken, eh?"

Callender stared at the woman. "They really meant to kill her, just because her husband was dead. And she was willing!"

"The promise of paradise, old boy. These Hindus promise each other paradise for any damned thing. I told you they were mad."

"That man," said Callender. "Who was he? What did he say to you?"

"That was her brother-in-law. His name is Ramjoy Ghosh, and he arranged this little party to honor his brother's memory. He said he hadn't done anything wrong, that the suttee was their custom." Hawke smiled. "And I told him that it was our custom to deal harshly with people who burn women alive."

Hawke wheeled his horse around and prepared to lead his party and their prisoners back to Dum Dum. "What is her name?" Callender called after him.

"Sarala. Sarala Ghosh."

Callender repeated the name to himself as he watched the others ride away. He lingered for a moment by the funeral pyre in spite of the infernal heat, contemplating the flames as they consumed all that remained of Sarala's husband. The smoldering shape pleased him; he was happy that the man was dead. In fact, he could not tear his eyes away. The blackened skeleton's form wavered in the smoke and seemed to turn into the body of the man he sought. He wondered if fire would truly destroy Sebastian Newcastle, or indeed if anything could. Callender thought about death. He tried to remember how many lives he had taken himself, but all of that was like the dim dream of another existence. And in any case, as he constantly reminded himself, none of that had been his fault.

And yet more than a little time elapsed before he could leave the fire burning on the banks of the Hooghly.

Two days passed before Callender saw Sarala Ghosh again, two days during which he seethed with frustration, for his old friend Lieutenant Hawke had grown distant, as aloof and officious as any other representative of the East India Company. They had refused to aid Callender in his quest, and now Hawke seemed to be one of them. In fact, he would not see Callender at all. There was nothing for the furious Callender to do but wander aimlessly through the streets of Calcutta, as if he hoped that he might come across Sebastian Newcastle lurking behind a building or hiding in a crowd.

Not even the heat of a steamboat's engine room had prepared Callender for the exhausting, enervating climate of the city, where the tar on the few paved roads actually melted in the midday sun. Almost immediately he adopted the Army's policy of confining his activity to the early morning and late evening hours. He knew now that Ramjoy Ghosh had scheduled the suttee for the afternoon because it was a good bet that no Englishmen would venture outside at that time. His nocturnal prowlings suited Callender for another reason, of course: the monster he was pursuing never came forth into the light of day.

As he wandered through the center of the city, his clothing soaked with sweat even in the comparative coolness after sunset, Callender could not help feeling a certain disappointment in his surroundings. Ridiculous as it might be, he admitted to himself that he had envisioned India as the sort of magical kingdom where his vengeance might take on truly heroic dimensions, a land of spires and minarets straight out of *The Arabian Nights*. Instead he saw only English architecture: gray office buildings and brick warehouses, with an occasional touch of the Gothic or the Greek. Nothing but the heat convinced him that he was not in London or Liverpool, but in a sense Calcutta really was an English city, for no native of India would have tried to build a metropolis in such a hellhole.

What finally pulled Callender out of his growing melancholy was a summons from Hawke, a message delivered to the sweltering hotel that was the cheapest he could find. In a sane world Callender would have hailed a cab, but in Calcutta he was obliged to make do with a rickshaw, a ridiculous little two-wheeled cart that was pulled by a man instead of a horse. Initially Callender felt a twinge of guilt over traveling in such a fashion, but long before he reached Dum Dum he wished he had a whip.

Again he was amazed at the size of Dum Dum; he had heard it called a station or an arsenal, and Lieutenant Hawke referred to it as the cantonment, but to Callender it looked like a small city, complete with its own bazaar. As he rolled past this section, he had only a glimpse of the countless stalls and shops which housed everything from candy makers to horse traders, but the noise and the stench were so intense that he was happy to pass by. The area where the Indian troops were quartered was scarcely more fragrant; here the tightly packed huts of mud and bamboo were separated by narrow trenches that were nothing more than open sewers.

Relieved to finally reach the more spacious and civilized area where the English officers and men were housed, Callender dismissed the rickshaw with the irritable feeling that he had been overcharged, then looked around for the second time. Again Hawke's invitation had been for the middle of the afternoon, and again the cantonment looked deserted, as if every one of the East India Company's men had been wiped out by some ghastly tropical disease. A glance at the extensive burial ground gave Callender the eerie feeling that this fantasy was not far from the truth, and the sight of the Anglican church made him think once more that the world was out of joint, that something had been yanked out of time and space that had no business there under India's white-hot sun.

It took him a few minutes to find Hawke's bungalow, hidden among countless others of similar design, but the frightened servant who lay on the veranda, working the punkah with his toe, was as good as a brass nameplate. And nearby a native soldier held two horses, Hawke's spirited chestnut and the old gray that Callender had borrowed on the day when he had first seen Sarala Ghosh. Wondering if he might ever encounter her again, Callender

85

mounted the porch and rapped on the open door. Lieutenant Hawke waved him in without rising from his wicker chair, while at the same time he took a long drink from a glass full of cracked ice and whiskey. Callender, who had expected to concern himself with other things, discovered that he could not take his eyes off the glass.

"What's the matter?" asked Hawke. "Surprised to see me drinking in the afternoon?"

"It's not the whiskey," said Callender through lips that suddenly turned dry, "it's the ice. Where did you get ice?"

"Oh, that. It comes in on ships from America. Whole ships full of ice, and hardly any of it melts. Remarkable, eh? Have some?"

To Callender, after his stint as a stoker in the tropics, the notion of a frozen ship conjured up visions of paradise, and while he luxuriated in an Arctic of the imagination, Hawke pulled a handful of blue-white crystals out of an old teakettle and dropped them into a glass.

Callender gritted his teeth. "Just that will do," he said. "No whiskey." He snatched at the glass, then smeared its contents across his lips and over the back of his neck.

"Well, suit yourself, but that's not much of a way to celebrate."

Callender shivered, his mind in a frigid cell on the outskirts of London. "What have I got to celebrate?"

"Just that," Hawke replied, tapping on the tabletop with a well-manicured forefinger.

Callender saw nothing but an old handkerchief, and after a moment he said so.

"Suppose that were Mr. Newcastle's linen," Hawke suggested.

"Nonsense. How can you tell? Is there a monogram?"

"Pick it up, old fellow."

Callender followed his instructions but was not enlightened. When he dropped the handkerchief, however, it landed on the table with a muffled rattle.

"You see?" smirked Hawke.

"See what?"

"There's a silver coin tied up in the end of that."

"It would have to be a ruby to interest me."

Lieutenant Hawke sighed and took another drink. "You're an amazing specimen. A perfect griffin, with nothing in your brain except revenge. I have to give you credit for being fool enough to come so far knowing so little."

"What are you talking about? What's a griffin?"

"A griffin is a new boy in India, and you're their champion, if you ask me. Don't you even know what you're looking for? That's what they call a rumel."

"Call it anything you like."

"They use the coin, you see, to get a grip on one end while they wrap the other end around your throat."

"What? Who does? Where did you get this?"

"That's right," Hawke intoned, like a man talking to a backward child. "It isn't Newcastle—I don't even know if there is a Newcastle—but I've caught a Thug."

Callender dropped his glass.

"Amazing coincidence, really," Hawke went on, "finding one so soon after you showed up with that story. Almost like destiny or something, don't you think? And quite a feather in my cap. I had a good mind to keep you out of it, but then I thought perhaps you were the one who brought me luck. It's been years since anyone's run into a Thug, and then one shows up the day after you arrive looking for 'em. Sure you wouldn't like a drink now, Callender?"

"Who was it? It wasn't the woman?"

"Sarala Ghosh? I saw you looking at her. Quite a hand-

87

some specimen, don't you think? But this wasn't hers. We found it in the possession of her husband's brother, Ramjoy Ghosh. Of course that does nothing to improve her position, but right now we think she could be innocent. Would you like some more ice?''

"Damn your ice! What have the authorities done with this Ramjoy Ghosh?''

"Authorities?'' Hawke leaned back in his wicker chair and closed his eyes. "There are no authorities. This was much too good to pass on to anyone. You are gazing at the man's judge, jury, and executioner.''

"You haven't killed him?'' Callender wailed.

"Not yet, but he's as good as dead, really. He just won't talk. They're all religious fanatics, you see, and they think if they're loyal, this big-breasted black woman called Kali will take them to heaven. They just won't talk.''

"You've been torturing him?''

"Just a bit. Sit down, will you? You're making me quite uncomfortable with all that posturing. You see, we have these men called Sikhs. They're not from this area, and they don't love Hindus. I have several of them, employed by the military but actually working for me. They're loyal as dogs, and they've done some interesting things to this man Ghosh. I would've thought the hookah would have done for him, actually.''

"Hookah?'' Callender tried to remember. "Isn't that some sort of pipe?''

"That's right. For smoking opium. They say it drives them mad if they can't get it, once they're used to it.'' Hawke smiled and leaned forward. "Something like whiskey, I suppose.''

Callender froze for a second, then methodically lifted Hawke's bottle and swallowed several ounces. He burned and choked without any outward sign, and then felt a glow that had eluded him for the best part of a year. "So you're taking your own prisoners, Hawke. What about Queen and country?"

"Queen and country are there to give me a leg up, my dear chum. Just like the opium trade. That's where I'd put my money, if I were you. It's where mine is. And the rest of my bets are on the Thugs, so don't forget who's running this show." Without any more warning, he picked up the teakettle and flung its contents into Callender's face. A shard of ice ripped a gash into Callender's cheek.

"That's right," Hawke continued, "I have my own little East India Company here. Why else would a man come to this godforsaken place? And why would I give a Thug up to the colonel when finding a nest of them would make me a hero? Not that I think it's going to work, mind you. I'm not a dreamer like you. Ramjoy Ghosh won't talk, but I thought it would be sporting to give you a look at him while he's still alive . . . You've got blood on your face, you know. Wipe it off."

The area by the bank of the Hooghly was uncomfortably familiar. A scorched spot was visible, and Callender wondered what had become of the body he had seen roasting there. Hawke, who was more familiar with local customs, simply assumed that it had come to rest in the river where thousands of corpses, burned and unburned, found their final burial ground. This was the same water which the people of Calcutta drank; it was the same water in which they bathed. And yet they thought cholera came from the gods.

Callender forgot the missing body at the moment when he beheld Sarala Ghosh. He had tried not to think of her at all, but when he had, circumstances forced him to imagine her as the bloody victim of Hawke and his mysterious

Sikhs. Instead, he found a vision of cool elegance in a white sari. The woman was unruffled, expressionless, well groomed. And the mark on her forehead, which he had failed to notice before, now told him she was a member of the highest Hindu caste, part of the nobility of Bengal.

By contrast, her brother-in-law might have been mistaken for the worst of the street beggars that Callender had encountered in his wanderings through the city. He was filthy, half naked, and covered with the rust-colored stripes that were the legacy of the lash. His hair and beard were matted with dried blood, one of his eyes was swollen shut, and most of his teeth were missing. He stood, weak-kneed, between two dark and burly men who remained imperturbable in the furnace of the afternoon, although they were rigged out in full uniforms of heavy twill.

Lieutenant Hawke's blond mustache seemed to spread out as he smiled, and his monocle caught the sunlight like a mirror when he turned his head toward the horses which were pulling a heavy cannon into the clearing. He grasped a handful of the prisoner's hair and yanked him around so he could see what was coming.

"You know what that's for, don't you, Ramjoy Ghosh? And don't pretend you don't understand English. I know better." Hawke drew back his hand as if to strike the man, watched him flinch, and smiled again. Callender remembered the bully's trick from his school days.

"I've wasted all the time I can with you," continued Hawke. "You and this woman have something to tell me about Thugs, and since you don't seem inclined to speak, I've decided to use you to give her a demonstration. You're about to be blown away, Ramjoy Ghosh, and nothing will save your body or your soul unless you speak at once."

The battered man's eyes rolled toward the cannon, but he clamped his mouth shut.

"You're not going to kill him?" protested Callender.

"I'm going to do much worse than that, my dear fellow. Most of these people don't really mind dying, don't you see, since they're so sure of paradise. This one thinks Kali will reward him. But there's no reward for a man who goes to his grave in pieces, is there, Ramjoy Ghosh? Your goddess will have nothing to do with a man who isn't whole, and there won't be enough left of you to pick up if you insist on keeping silent. Why not turn approver and let the others in your band die instead of you? It's only sensible."

Ramjoy Ghosh fixed his eyes on Callender as if he expected mercy from that quarter. "I have a wife and children," he murmured hoarsely.

"You see?" trumpeted Hawke. "I told you he spoke English. And isn't it remarkable how these fellows think they have the right to do anything they please just because they have a wife and children? Well, if it's true that he has them, they'll no doubt be better off without him. Take him over to the gun!"

The two Sikhs dragged their prisoner down an incline to the spot where another pair of men were already busy making adjustments to the cannon. Hawke sauntered after them, hacking at some dry grass with his riding crop, and Sarala slowly followed him. Callender wondered why she was not under guard herself, although he doubted if she could really hope to run from so many armed men. She certainly did not have the air of a captive, but perhaps that was not in her nature.

He hurried to catch up with Hawke. "You can't kill him. I must talk to him. He may know something!"

"I'm sure he knows a great deal, but he's not inclined to share it with us."

"I mean about Newcastle!"

"Of course you do. But there's nothing left that might

make him speak now except the uncomfortable moment when he finds himself tied to the mouth of that eighteen pounder. And once he's there, my men will lose all respect for me unless I blow him away.''

''Damn you, Hawke. I believe you enjoy torturing me as much as you do that miserable assassin.''

''Well, after all, you said you were a convicted murderer yourself, didn't you? But I'll give you a chance with him just before we're ready to fire. It's the best time, really. You can have a minute.''

A bird of some sort cried out in the nearby thicket of palm trees as the Sikh soldiers tied Ramjoy Ghosh's arms to the barrel of the gun behind him, the muzzle resting between his shoulder blades. The cannon, over seven feet in length, had been aimed toward the river, and one of Hawke's men stood behind it with a smoldering length of cord ready in his hand.

Hawke was holding something round and heavy. He clutched it in both hands and thrust it toward Ramjoy Ghosh's eyes. ''You see that? Do you? That's an eighteen-pound ball. It might not be the biggest one you've ever seen—in fact, it's not quite as big as your head. No doubt you think we should have had a team of elephants drag out one of our biggest fieldpieces to attend to you, but I promise you that a ball this size is quite enough to tear you apart. There's one just behind you ready to be fired, and there's a man ready to put the spark to the vent. As far as I'm concerned, you are already dead, but there's someone who wants a minute of your time, and unless you answer his questions, it will be your last minute on earth.''

Ramjoy Ghosh engaged in rapid theological speculations for which he had not been trained. He knew that the impact of the eighteen pounder would condemn his spirit to an eternity of aimless wandering, but that betraying his comrades would surely bring down the wrath of Kali, which might be even worse. He had reached a state of such fear and such bewilderment that he could only pray for some sort of omen, a flight of birds or the roar of a beast.

What he got instead was a ragged Englishman with a sandy beard who whispered to him in an undertone. "For God's sake, man, just answer. We can't let the woman see something like this, can we?"

Ramjoy Ghosh stared at him in utter bewilderment. Callender raised his voice. "What do you know of Sebastian Newcastle?"

"What?" wailed Ramjoy Ghosh indignantly. "What are you talking about?"

"All right," Callender continued nervously. "Perhaps that's not his name, but you know who I mean. The tall pale man who does magic. The one who looks for Kali. The dead man. The one with the scar."

Callender felt that the interrogation was not going well. The prisoner was glancing wildly from side to side like a broken puppet. The whole affair seemed suddenly like some sort of childish game, thought Callender, with Hawke a toy soldier in a ridiculous plumed helmet, and Sarala only a pretty doll in a flowing white robe. Callender tried to shake off the impression. "You know who I mean," he said in a confidential tone. "The man who drinks blood."

Ramjoy Ghosh tried to find some meaning in all this, but his brain was numb with panic. "This man is mad!" he shouted. "These are not proper questions!"

"Quite right," observed Lieutenant Hawke, unceremoniously pulling Callender toward the rear of the cannon. "It's all a complete waste of time." He nodded toward his men.

"Fire," he drawled.

Ramjoy Ghosh twisted his head around, his face dripping with sweat, to gaze upon the smoke and spark of flaming gunpowder. He felt a fierce itch between his shoulder blades. "Wait!" he screamed to the cannon. "Ask me now!"

"Wait!" screamed Callender. "He knows!"

Their cries for more time were cut short by an explosion that left Callender's ears ringing, and his eyes blinded by smoke that reeked of sulphur. Something struck the ground near his feet with a heavy thud.

Callender coughed twice, and as the smoke began to clear he saw that what had landed near him was the head of Ramjoy Ghosh, with most of the neck and part of one shoulder still attached. The face showed no expression, but where it had struck the earth, the dust had mixed with perspiration to form a thin mask of mud. For some reason it was this detail that sent the sour bile of Callender's stomach crawling up his throat. He choked it back, determined not to disgrace himself by vomiting in front of the woman.

The head of Ramjoy Ghosh had been thrown backward by the impact of the cannonball, and the arms lay on each side of the gun at a distance of several yards. The legs had fallen in a tangle beneath the cannon's mouth, but there was no sign of the torso except for a puddle of blood and a few chunks which Callender chose not to identify. Under the sharp sting of the gunpowder was another odor, much less antiseptic.

A fly buzzed from the red ruin toward Callender's face, and he battered it away as if he feared for his life.

"Remarkable how easily one comes apart," allowed Lieutenant Hawke. "I remember being quite shocked the first time I saw it."

Suddenly Callender was reminded of Sarala Ghosh. If

he had found this experience horrifying, what must it have been like for her, when the victim was a member of her own family?

"You should never have done that in front of the woman," Callender declared.

"Why not?" asked Sarala Ghosh. "My husband's brother would have been quite happy to watch me burn to death."

Callender was hearing her voice for the first time. Its tone was low and musical, and her English was perfect, but for some reason, he could not quite grasp the meaning of what she said. He supposed he must look like a fool, because Hawke began to laugh. The woman stood beside him.

"But you went willingly into that fire," stammered Callender. "I saw you."

Sarala answered him with a grave smile. "That was only prudent," she replied. "Otherwise my husband's family would have forced me into the flames, and they might have done me an injury."

Callender glanced once more at the thing on the ground and then stepped away from it. "I don't understand," he said.

"You mustn't assume that everyone in India's a superstitious savage," Hawke told him, "least of all Sarala Ghosh. I told you we learned about that suttee from an informant, but I suppose I did neglect to give you her name."

"Some widows die willingly," said Sarala, "but I am not that kind. Others are forced, but I am not that kind either. And since the suttee is against the English law, what I did was only justice."

"So she was true to England, and true to India too," said Hawke. "Truly an admirable woman."

Callender felt somehow betrayed. He had not expected the serene Sarala Ghosh to be quite so cold-blooded. "Then she knows about the Thugs!" he exclaimed.

"No," she replied. "I do not."

"I suppose you might be right, old fellow, come to think of it. I was inclined to believe her story, but she certainly has shown she's capable of deception. I wonder what she'd say if I had her tied to that cannon."

"Surely you won't do that!" protested Callender, his gaze shifting rapidly from Hawke to the woman to the cannon. The four Sikhs were smiling and chatting among themselves like men at a party.

"I told you that I know nothing of the Thugs," Sarala insisted. "If I wanted to protect them, would I have given you my husband's brother?"

"You might have," said Hawke, "to save your own neck. I admit it's a pretty neck, and you're obviously fond of it. I think just a touch of that gun's barrel might transform you into a veritable fount of information."

"But you couldn't do something that brutal to a woman," said Callender.

"It's bit late to worry about brutality now," said Hawke. He glanced at what was left of Ramjoy Ghosh.

Callender contemplated the same ugly objects. The thought of turning Sarala into such wreckage brought back unwholesome memories, and these in turn inspired him to fear and fury. "But if she doesn't know anything, then she can't talk, and you'd kill her anyway! For nothing!"

"All strategy involves an element of risk," said Hawke.

The woman was silent and motionless. Callender felt quite dizzy from the heat. A cloud of fat black flies swarmed around the cannon, and as he watched, a scrawny vulture floated down to join them. It plucked at a piece of something stringy with its filthy beak, and Callender let out a groan. Without even realizing what he meant to do, he yanked the revolver from Hawke's belt and fired at the bird. There was a flash of blood and a flurry of feathers.

The four Sikhs looked at the crazy Englishman, and Callender looked at the pistol in his hand.

"A good shot," drawled Hawke, "and you thought you weren't bloodthirsty. Oh, by the way, you'd better let me have that back now."

Callender did not move.

"The pistol, if you please," Hawke said a little more sharply. "Government issue." The sun turned his monocle into a blaze of light.

"I don't think so," said Callender, raising the pistol until it was aimed at the gleaming glass in Hawke's right eye. "I think I'll keep it."

One of the Sikhs raised his musket, but lowered it again when Hawke gave an order that Callender could not understand.

"Tell your men to put their weapons down," Callender said. "No. Tell them to throw them into the river."

"They won't do it, old fellow. Those are their most precious possessions."

"They'll do it," said Callender, gesturing with the revolver. "You tell them."

Hawke gave the order, and Callender watched the Sikhs trudge angrily toward the bank of the Hooghly. He beckoned Sarala to his side and put his left arm around her. She never spoke. Her flesh felt hotter than the sun.

"Now tell them to drive the horses away. All but that chestnut you ride."

"My dear fellow! What do you hope to gain by all this?"

"I don't know. But it feels good. It feels better than watching you strut. Watching you give orders, and kill prisoners, and threaten women. I like it. I like having a gun. Now, do what I said about the horses.''

It was clear that the Sikhs could scarcely believe their ears when they heard the orders, but they could see the gun at their lieutenant's head, and before long their own mounts, the gun horses, and even Callender's old gray were cantering away along the riverbank.

''You stay close to me now, old childhood chum,'' Callender told Hawke as he backed toward the one remaining horse, his arm still cradling the woman with black eyes and golden skin. He had to release her to mount the chestnut, a maneuver that was clumsy enough with one hand holding a pistol, but an English gentleman knows how to handle horses if he knows nothing else, and Callender had been a gentleman less than a year ago. He could hardly believe what he was doing now, pointing a gun at an old friend on the edge of a jungle and helping a native woman up into the saddle in front of him. She sat well, he noticed, and the touch of her body against his was like fire.

The Sikhs stood grouped together menacingly by the river. Callender was sure that at least one of them had a knife hidden in his clothing, but he doubted if one could be thrown far enough to hit him. The eighteen pounder was pointed away from him, and he doubted if they could turn it fast enough to do him or Sarala any harm. Callender looked down at Hawke and started to speak, but realized he had nothing to say.

''Going for a ride, old man?'' asked Hawke. ''Where to?''

''I don't know. But I'm going to get this woman away from you, and I'm going to find Sebastian Newcastle.''

''They were right about you, you know. You are mad.''

Callender's reply was almost a reflex. He kicked out with his left foot and caught Hawke full in the face, sending him sprawling in the dust. The chestnut snorted and wheeled around.

"There's blood on your face," said Callender. "You'd better put some ice on it!"

He dug his heels into the chestnut's ribs and it bolted off into the trees. The Sikhs rushed forward and Callender fired a shot over their heads. Then he and Sarala were gone.

Lieutenant Christopher Hawke sat in the dirt and rubbed his jaw. Two of his men helped him to his feet while the others ran downriver in search of the horses. Hawke brushed himself off and stared into the jungle.

"I'll be damned," he said. And then he began to laugh.

# *E I G H T*

# *The Shrine*

North of Calcutta, and north of the Dum Dum arsenal as well, in the marsh and mud and jungle that surround the Hooghly River, the ancient shrine to the dark goddess stood. So long ago had it been raised that only those dead for uncounted centuries could have remembered when the first of its stones was carved, and so long had it been abandoned, by those who knew Calcutta but had forgotten the old village of Kalikata, that only the creatures of the wild gazed upon it, and only moss and vines climbed up its time-stained steps.

If truly this was where the severed finger of the dead goddess fell, then the shrine itself might have been that gigantic finger, the stump rooted in the damp earth with only the topmost joint exposed, for the stone spire rose straight up for half its height, and then the sides tapered inward to form a curved peak. The four sides of the structure, which was square at the bottom yet round at the top,

100

were ribbed with deep-cut grooves between which upright curved columns rose, and each of these was marked horizontally into innumerable small sections, intricately decorated by the stonecutter's art. The doorway echoed the shrine's shape in miniature, and it was flanked by the smiling shapes of stylized crocodiles, while above the arch, on either side, reclined the figures of a pair of naked women, incredibly voluptuous at breast and hip, yet incredibly slim at the waist. Tiny monkeys kept the women company, and in fact, there were stone figures nestled all over the surface of the shrine.

All of this had been clearly visible to Sebastian as they had approached the structure for the first time, whereas Jamini, half mad with giddiness after his first flight in his own demon's claws, and no more blessed than any other mortal with the power to see at night, had perceived no more than a dark mass as tall as seven men.

Kalidas Sen had led them inside, into the empty stone chamber whose vaulted ceiling echoed to their footsteps, and then to the weighted block which turned at the proper touch to reveal a passage that led down into the earth. Then he had left them alone in a darkness that was blacker than any night.

Jamini sat on the floor, his back against wet rock, and gazed into emptiness. The air beneath the shrine, what there was of it, made him think of something that had been dead for a long time. If not for Sebastian's presence, he would have been afraid.

"Will we fly again soon?" the boy asked.

"Perhaps," was the only answer from the darkness, and Jamini realized he would have to wait and see.

"Is the goddess here?" he asked after a little time had passed.

"She was here once, and she will be here again. If she is gone, it is because men have forgotten her."

"I mean the other one. The golden goddess. Can you see her, Sebastian?"

"I see her."

"What is she like?"

"She is dancing."

"Dancing! Is she happy, then?"

"I suppose she is happy, for she is standing on a corpse, and its head is in one of her hands."

"And in her other hand?"

"One of them holds a sword, but she has four hands, boy."

"Four! And what are the other two doing?"

"They are empty. Yet one seems to be offering something, and the other seems to soothe."

"Then we should not be afraid of her, even if she stands on a corpse?"

"The corpse means nothing. It is the void, the emptiness that is beyond time and matter, and this is what sustains the goddess. For those who come to her, who accept the boundless bliss that is eternity, who renounce the illusion of the world, there is nothing to fear from her."

"I don't understand you. Did she tell you all this?"

"I learn by looking at her, Jamini."

"I wish I could see her too. Is she really made of gold? How is she dressed?"

"She is gold. And she is naked, save for her headdress and her jewelry. Her necklace is made of human skulls."

The boy closed his eyes, which was hardly necessary, and tried to imagine her. After a while the effort tired him and he gave it up. He sat and thought.

"Are you English, Sebastian? You dress like an Englishman, and you talk like an Englishman, but I do not think you are one.''

''I am not. I came from another country, but that was long ago. Now I am from nowhere.''

''Like Kali?''

''We shall see.''

''I am glad you are not English. Is Sebastian Newcastle your real name?''

''Once it was Don Sebastian de Villanueva, but it means much the same thing.''

''Then I will call you Sebastian Newcastle, as long as you are not really English.''

''Good. Are you breathing, boy? Is there enough air for you?''

''It smells bad, but there is air.''

''Then go to sleep, Jamini, and when you wake tomorrow, you may look at the goddess. But be sure you stay here until I rise. Then the silk merchant will come, and he will bring us food. Until then we will be hungry, so sleep as long as you can.''

When Jamini opened his eyes again, the room under the shrine of Kali seemed almost as dark as it had before, but some light was seeping in from somewhere, for slowly his eyes grew accustomed to the gloom, and he could see things in it. The first was the shape of the woman with four arms, her sword gleaming dully in a narrow ribbon of dim light that evidently dropped through a crack in the ceiling above. There was nothing else in the square room, whose rough-hewn stone walls sweated water from the surrounding swamp, except of course for Sebastian, and he was dead.

That did not worry the boy, however, for he had seen Sebastian dead every day, and seen him rise again every night, just as all things that died were given life again. Even the silk merchant knew about that.

What did worry Jamini was that small beam of gray light that shone on Kali's sword. A little thing like that might cause a big problem. It hardly looked like light from the sun, but Jamini knew he had to keep his demon away from the glow of the day at all costs. That was what the box was for, but the box was still on its way here from the city, unless Kalidas Sen had forgotten it. The boy thanked the goddess for letting the light fall on her instead of on Sebastian, then took hold of the demon's long black hair and dragged him into the corner that was farthest from the statue.

Then there was nothing for him to do but wait.

He looked at Kali and tried to see the stories that Sebastian saw in her, but all he could see was a naked woman made of gold, so he made up stories for himself about what he would do if he met a naked woman, and what he would do if he had all that gold. Yet he was almost certain that these were not the right kinds of stories, unless there was a way for a boy to worship Kali by thinking only of his own pleasure.

When he was tired of worrying about that, Jamini began to worry about Sebastian. It was better than thinking about food. The boy was worried because there was no way he could be sure that Kali would like Sebastian as much as she should, and he was even more concerned about Kalidas Sen, because it was one of the few unswerving principles of Jamini's brief experience that no one who sold things was to be trusted. What would happen if the silk merchant came early and found Sebastian helpless? What would he do? Should he even know?

All at once the boy decided that he could not take the chance of letting anyone enter the shrine before sunset. He hurried to the short flight of steps beside the goddess and clambered up them, realizing as he did so that the faint crack of light came from an opening at the top. It would no doubt be a simple matter to find the way out now, but it was not. Jamini pushed against the square stone with all his strength and found that he could not move it. He felt for a hinge like the one on Sebastian's box, his quick fingers running along the edges and even the surface of the stone, but he discovered nothing. He pushed again. He struck at the unyielding obstacle with both his fists until they bled. He cursed the rock, he shouted, and he even began to cry. Now that he was trapped inside, he was certain that he must get out to protect Sebastian. He slumped against the rock, sobbing, and as he did, the counterbalance gave way and he sprawled out into the vaulted chamber of the shrine.

He gasped with relief, rubbed his eyes, and then shook off his shame. Only after he was free did it occur to him that he had never thought to ask the goddess for help, but there was nothing he could do about that now. He ran out into the afternoon.

The jungle heat struck him with the force of a blow. The secret shadowed chamber where Sebastian still rested had been cool if nothing else, but Jamini was glad to exchange it for fresh air, however thick with humidity it was. He longed to venture out into the jungle, to look for animals, to find a mango tree with its juicy yellow fruit, but he was here as a guardian, and he would not betray his trust. He glanced up at the spire looming over him and then turned his back on it, for the figures of the women over the doorway were not as beautiful as Kali was.

He sat on the steps and waited, and things came to pass as he had suspected they would, for Kalidas Sen arrived at the shrine while there was still light in the sky. The silk merchant rode a scruffy gray packhorse, its back also laden with bags and bundles of various shapes and sizes. He looked more than ever like a peddler, but the boy knew that what the horse carried was not for sale. Kalidas Sen dismounted and walked toward him.

"You have come too soon," Jamini said.

"I am ardent. What is that to you?"

"You should not have come before night. He will be angry with you."

"I'll go in and talk to him about it."

"No. If you do, he will be angry with me."

"What? Would you keep me out of my own shrine?"

"It is not yours. It is Kali's."

The leader of the Thugs wore a loose black shirt and baggy black trousers, reminding Jamini of the night when he was nearly strangled. The man's thick lips twitched, and his heavy eyebrows snaked together into a sinister scowl. He raised his right hand.

Jamini did not flinch. "I tell you for your own good to wait for nightfall. Sebastian has commanded it, and he could kill you with a look. He is a demon of great power."

"And you are a boy of great impudence," declared Kalidas Sen, but nonetheless he lowered his hand. Without another word he stepped over to his horse and began to unpack it.

"What have you got there?" Jamini asked him.

"That which is needed for the ceremony."

"What ceremony?"

"You will see after nightfall."

Jamini took a moment to digest this information, then spoke again. "Did you bring me something to eat?"

Kalidas Sen took on the appearance of one who wished that he could kill with a look as easily as a demon could, then sighed and opened one of his bundles. "I have some

106

of that almond paste candy you like," he said, "and some bananas and some figs."

The boy devoured the candy first, then peeled a banana. A little monkey scampered down from one side of the shrine and sat making plaintive noises at a safe distance from the intruders into his domain. Jamini glanced up to make sure this was not one of the stone monkeys come to life, then smiled and tossed the creature a piece of the fruit.

"I didn't carry that for miles so you could feed it to animals," said the silk merchant.

"You didn't carry it at all. An animal did. Where is Sebastian's box?"

"It is coming later; I came early because I wanted to speak to Sebastian. We have plans to make."

"He doesn't need you for that."

Lowering himself down to a step not too close to the boy, Kalidas Sen sat and brooded. A ripple in the nearby grass told him that a snake was passing by, and he toyed with the idea of snatching it up and throwing it at Jamini. Kalidas Sen had nothing to fear from snakes, not even cobras, and if the boy were killed, Sebastian might believe it had been an accident.

He decided there was too much risk in trying to fool Sebastian, but he longed for a cobra anyway. If a boy could make friends with a monkey, why should a man not make friends with cobras? Monkeys were foolish, but serpents were full of wisdom, and they imparted this wisdom to those who sought them out. They gave a man visions, if he had the courage to face their bite and the cunning to expose himself to the venom gradually. The silk merchant had learned this years ago, and now the cobra was his opium, his bhang. His body was covered with the faded marks of fangs, and in his serpent dreams he had seen the goddess dance. Here in the secret shrine his father had shown him, Kali had promised her namesake, Kalidas Sen, that he would have riches and power once he took up the rumel and found others who would do the same, and so it had been. Yet now the goddess had given him more than he had requested. Surely her generosity was to be praised, but what was he to do with Sebastian Newcastle?

"Why is Kali naked?" asked the boy.

The silk merchant was jolted back into the moment. He glanced around, blinking at the long shadows of the trees and the gray of twilight.

"What? You are talking nonsense, boy."

"But why is she naked?"

"How should I know why she is naked? Because she is beautiful. Because she is proud. Because she is unafraid. Why would anyone be naked? You may be sure it is because she has chosen it, and not because she lacks for raiment, or for any other thing."

"The goddess has nothing," intoned a hollow voice behind them, "and she is dressed in nothing, because nothing is her element. This world is a veil, an illusion, and when the world is stripped away, the veil is gone and there is only naked truth."

Kalidas Sen whirled around to find Sebastian standing in the entrance to the shrine. "You are right, of course," murmured the leader of the Thugs, "and I would have said that, but I did not think the boy would understand."

Still garbed in the heavy black suit of the detested English, Sebastian Newcastle inclined his head. "Yet you are also right," he acknowledged with grave courtesy, "for surely she is beautiful, and proud, and unafraid."

The silk merchant was surprised to feel his face grow flush with an embarrassed satisfaction; he could only bow his head in turn.

Sebastian surveyed the world outside the shrine. "That horse should be hidden," he declared.

"I would have taken her inside, but the boy would not let me pass."

"He is a good boy," Sebastian said, and Jamini grinned.

"I suppose he is, but I was in a hurry. I have much to tell you."

"Then you will tell me now. Jamini, take the horse into the shrine and tend to her. Wait for us there."

Kalidas Sen stared out into the darkness of the surrounding jungle as if he expected to see something come out of it. "Your box will be here soon. Some of my men are bringing it. And something else, if they have obeyed me. I hope it will please you."

"I hope so too, master of Thugs."

Kalidas Sen looked at the ground. "So much is happening so fast," he said. "There is no time."

"Kali is the mistress of time, and for her there is neither sooner nor later. There is only the now, which is eternity."

"Then may the goddess help us. I told you of a Thug who died. Now the English have arrested his bride and his brother, and the brother was carrying the sacred handkerchief. He was a fool, but now he is dead. The woman is not."

"Will she speak?"

"Who can say? She is a silent woman, and she appears to be strong, but she is a stranger. I know nothing of her but that she may have the power to ruin us all."

"What is her name?"

"Sarala."

"Perhaps we shall see her soon. All this must be as the goddess intended. It is destiny."

"But why should the goddess send you to us, and send so much trouble at the same time?"

"We can only serve her and wait for a sign. And if it means death, remember that she rules death, and I have come from the dead to serve you."

There was a crackling of branches in the jungle before the shrine; even in the faint light of the quarter-moon Sebastian could see a group of black-clad men making their way through the trees. "They are carrying my box," he said. "But why is it so heavy?"

"That is as it should be."

"And there are so many men."

"I summoned them. They must realize our mission is more than to be thieves and murderers." Kalidas Sen paused for a moment to summon up his courage. "Will you take the boy below and wait for us? I want to prepare them for your presence."

Sebastian slipped back into the shrine without a word, but that seemed answer enough to the king of the Thugs, who rose to greet his followers with outstretched arms.

Sebastian hurried Jamini through the passage in the wall and down into the blackness of the cellar beneath the shrine. From above them came the sound of shuffling feet, and then a startling crash as something hard and heavy dropped to the floor. The murmur of voices rose, and above them sang the harsh tones of the silk merchant, exhorting the assembled Thugs with such enthusiasm that sometimes Jamini could make out the words even through a layer of stone:

> *Terror is Thy name, O Kali*
> *And Death is in Thy Hand.*
> *May Thy sword protect us*
> *As Thy hand comforts us.*

*Who dares love misery*
*And hugs the form of Death,*
*To him the Mother comes!*

There were shouts of assent to these sentiments, and then the shuffling began again. The stone block above the golden goddess opened wide, bathing the statue in a glow of firelight as Kalidas Sen descended with a torch held high. Behind him four men struggled with the coffin, which inhabitants of this district had little reason to recognize as such, and in their wake followed at least a dozen other Thugs, some bearing torches and others carrying offerings to the goddess: flowers, incense, bells, ornaments, and dishes of food.

Sebastian and Jamini stayed in the shadows behind the figure of Kali. When the boy saw the dishes of rice and curry and sweetmeats, his hand stretched out toward them almost instinctively, but Sebastian held him back. "Later," he whispered. "When these men are gone, the goddess will be glad to share with you."

"Prepare the offering for he whom Kali has sent to us," commanded the leader of the men as they placed their gifts before the shining statue. Two of the Thugs bent to open the coffin, and Kalidas Sen raised his torch as the lid swung back. He looked into the box.

"Fools!" he shouted. "This man is dead! I told you to bring an Englishman alive!"

"But he would not come alive!" said a voice from the crowd.

Sebastian emerged from his place behind the goddess, Jamini at his heels, and the men who surrounded the coffin made way for him. Some cringed as he passed, while others stared at him with avid curiosity. Sebastian took the torch from the trembling fingers of their leader.

111

The face of the man in the box was swollen and purple; his eyes were bulging and his tongue protruded almost impudently. The rumel was still tightly knotted around his throat. Jamini could not turn his eyes away. He had seen corpses before, but there was something about this one that fascinated him; perhaps it was the fact that the dead man's hair and beard were red. Jamini remembered such a man, one who had taught him a song some nights ago near the great temple in the city.

"The journalist," Sebastian said quietly. "Wakefield. So even you are part of Kali's plan. You should have left Calcutta when you intended to."

"I meant to have an offering for you," said Kalidas Sen. "A blood sacrifice." His hands made a futile gesture; then he turned to face his men. "Which one of you killed him?" he roared.

No one answered him, but each of the Thugs moved away from one of their band as if they thought he had contracted leprosy.

"You should not have killed this man," Kalidas Sen told the guilty one.

"I never meant to. He was drunk. It looked easy, but he fought like a tiger! I had to kill him!"

"And then you took his money. And you did not give it to me to share with the others."

"I only did what Kali told us to do."

"Then explain it to her, for I will have no more of you!"

With a strength born of fury, Kalidas Sen grasped the man by the shoulders and hurled him across the torchlit room toward the statue of Kali, then yanked him off his feet and jammed his upturned throat against the dancing figure's heavy golden sword. A scarlet shower sprayed across the room, raining down on the food and flowers at the statue's feet, as Kalidas Sen spun the dying man around and thrust him toward Sebastian.

"I swore that you would feast tonight," cried the leader of the Thugs, while his men cringed and hid their eyes from this abominable sacrilege.

"No blood spilled!" they shouted. "No blood spilled!" And while their voices echoed off the stone walls of the shrine, the fountain of life splashed into Sebastian's dead mouth.

In the space of a few heartbeats the butchered Thug gave up the ghost; his blood no longer gushed. Sebastian, his face a red mask with fathomless eyes, lifted up his head as if he had heard a voice calling him from far away. He turned toward the goddess, her golden flesh spotted with gore, and stared at her intently, as if some sort of message might be passing between them. Then his eyes shifted again, and it seemed to those around him that he was listening once more, responding to a summons that came from somewhere outside in the night.

He tossed aside the dead man and raced up the steps at an ungodly speed. He was gone in an instant, out of the shrine before the corpse he had discarded hit the floor.

Nobody spoke in the dark cellar, and nobody moved. The Thugs and their leader stood dumbstruck, not even responding when Jamini slipped out after his master before the secret stone could trap him once again. In the shadows of the vault the silk merchant's horse shied and snorted, a monster in the night. The boy rushed out of the shrine that stood against the sky like the severed stump of a gigantic finger. The monkeys on its walls chattered and shrieked at him.

Sebastian was nowhere in sight. The boy ran into the black jungle shouting his name.

## NINE

# The Black Panther

Earlier that evening, only a short while after riding off with Sarala in his arms, Reginald Callender had been forced to admit he was hopelessly lost. He was beginning to wonder if his romantic gesture might have been a mistake. The jungle in which they had become enmeshed was really more like a swamp, its bogs a constant menace to the passage of Hawke's chestnut stallion, and the stolen horse was soon transformed from a blessing to a burden. The only really solid ground seemed to lie by the banks of the river, but Callender realized they would be captured in short order if they followed the course of the Hooghly, especially since its winding length nurtured so many villages where strangers could be noticed. And so he had turned east, away from the water. He knew that he was north of Dum Dum, and still farther north of Calcutta; it seemed inevitable that he should continue to travel in that direction, away from the pursuit which was sure to come.

So man and woman and horse moved northeast: away from the river, away from civilization, and toward they knew not what.

Even as he did his best to elude Hawke and his men, Callender was conscious of a desire to be taken prisoner by them before this wilderness swallowed him up. Even the chilly confines of his cell in the madhouse might be preferable to death in this green inferno, where the ground was almost liquid and the air as nearly solid with swarms of insects. There were moths, white ants, crickets, and beetles, but the worst were the flies, with their incessant buzzing and their lust for carrion. More than once they drove him into a frenzy as they descended on him, so that he shouted and waved his arms as if they really could be driven away by such futile gestures. He would have been as well advised to battle with the breeze, but there was no breeze.

The woman by contrast was silent, stoic, yet she was visibly wilting in the oppressive heat, her damp hair clinging to the sides of her face, her white sari soaked with sweat. It was she who finally took mercy on their mount, slipping off his back and stepping ankle-deep into the marsh which entangled his hooves. "Sometimes walking is better than riding," she told Callender. "You will tire your horse less if you lead him."

Seeing the wisdom in this, Callender jumped down beside her and instantly felt water soaking into his boots. "I would be glad to lead him if I knew where to go," he said.

"Where did you intend to go?"

"I don't know. I only meant to get us away from there."

"But now you see that getting away means coming to another place."

"I did what I thought best," snapped Callender as a

grass tick burrowed into his leg. He stooped to scratch at it, suddenly ashamed. "I had to do something. They might have killed you. I didn't want to see pieces of you scattered on the ground."

"You could have turned your head away," said Sarala. "You may have wished me well, but I am already a dead woman."

"If Hawke catches up with us now, I may be dead myself."

"I meant something else. I died when my husband did."

Callender peered into her grave and enigmatic eyes. "You loved him that much?"

"I hated him. He was a fool, and so was his brother. But I was expected to follow him into death, and even now, when I have escaped his funeral pyre with a trick, I am dead to my family and my friends. To everyone. A widow is not much use in India. If I go home I will almost certainly be murdered, unless I am good enough to do the right thing by throwing myself into the river."

"I wouldn't do that if I were you. It's full of crocodiles."

Callender's remark was rewarded with what might have been a smile. "It is quicker to be eaten by crocodiles than by insects," Sarala said.

Callender nodded, took a step forward, and sank up to his knees. "Even the horse is not such an idiot as that," he said. He turned in another direction and became entangled in a thornbush. He pulled off his hat and threw it on the ground.

"They say Englishmen die in heat like this," Sarala informed him. "They just fall to the ground and shake, and then they die."

He retrieved his hat and found it somewhat more comfortable after the drenching it had received. An uncanny

116

noise came out of the jungle around them, a cross between a woman's scream and the sound of sawing wood. "A panther," Sarala said, and Callender reached for the pistol in his belt.

"They are most often shy of men," said Sarala, "and will even leave one they have wounded rather than stay to kill him."

"Small comfort in that," replied Callender, his hand still on the grip of the gun.

"And they rarely stir before nightfall. The hour must be growing late."

It was true. The overhanging foliage made judgment difficult, yet Callender could see, through the branches of the coconut palms and mango trees, that the sky was turning slowly scarlet. The sight brought a chill despite the heat of India. He had no wish at all to spend the night in such a place.

"We must find water," said the woman.

"Water? That's the one thing we don't lack, it seems to me."

"And yet we do. We need clean water, for drinking. And for bathing if we have the chance. The heat is our greatest enemy, and not Lieutenant Hawke."

"Hawke's canteen!" Callender pulled the stallion toward him and grabbed at the saddle. He found the small, canvas-covered container and gave it a shake, then smiled. "It's full," he said. He unscrewed the top and offered Sarala a drink.

"No," she said. "I cannot drink. It is for you."

"But you just said we needed water," Callender sputtered.

"I am a Brahmin, and I may not drink from any vessel that has been touched by this unbeliever Hawke."

"What? Is this some of that caste business? What does

117

that mean now? Is everybody in this country mad? How can you still cling to something like that when you tell me what an outcast you have become?''

"And are you not an outcast too? Yet I have heard an English gentleman is still a gentleman, even when he has no money and no friends. Would you spurn your principles for a few drops of water?''

"I am no gentleman," rasped Callender, yet he lifted up the canteen, still untasted, and hurled it into the trees.

"And you are no Brahmin," Sarala said. "You should have kept the water, Mr. Callender.''

"You may be right at that. Is there anything safe to eat in this damned jungle?''

"There are coconuts hanging over your head, if you can find a way to bring them down and break them open.''

He glanced up and ran a hand across his mouth. These were not honest English trees with branches men could climb on, but rough stalks with nothing to cling to but the bark. He hated the thought that he might fail to reach the top of one while the proud and lovely Sarala looked on. He hooked his hands in his belt, and it was then that inspiration struck. Without a word of warning he yanked out Hawke's revolver and fired up into the tree. The stallion shied and Sarala had to hold the reins to keep him from bolting.

Callender took three shots to bring down one coconut. In the back of his mind he realized that his behavior was inexcusably rash, but somehow he didn't care. Perhaps it was the heat. He even imagined that he might be half hoping he would attract pursuers with his noise, but principally he was aware of the supreme satisfaction that came when the coconut tumbled down out of the sky. It was neatly drilled, and thin sweet milk dribbled from the bullet hole. "There!" He grinned triumphantly. "Even a Brahmin can drink that!"

Sarala complied, but after Callender had stripped off the green husk and cracked the hairy shell with the butt of his gun, she refused his offer of the moist white meat. This time Callender decided to swallow his dignity along with the coconut. The food should have restored his confidence, he thought, but the time he had taken to consume it just brought the darkness that much closer.

"We can't spend the night out here," he said. "There must be some sort of shelter. Do you know anything about the country around here?"

"My skin may be darker than yours, but I have not spent my life in the jungle, Mr. Callender. We can find shelter along the river, but I think we will find your friend Lieutenant Hawke there too."

"He's no friend of mine. But I think you're right that he'll be looking for us, or at least for you. He's very keen on the subject of Thugs."

"And aren't you keen as well? I saw you questioning my husband's brother."

"I don't care anything about the Thugs. They can strangle anyone they like, for all of me. I'm just looking for one man, and I think he may be with them. I've followed him halfway around the world."

"Then he is your countryman?"

"I followed him from England, but he's no Englishman."

"I suppose you think no Englishman would bow down to Kali, but I know that the English are full of tricks."

"What do you mean by that?" asked Callender, his eyes shifting around as he looked for a path that might lead somewhere.

"When they wish to know something, one of them will

be cruel and harsh. Then another one will come along who pretends he is a friend, and he gets the secrets as a gift that his comrade could not extract by force.''

''So that's what you think of me, is it?''

Sarala's only answer was to turn her back and lead the stallion across what seemed to be a patch of solid ground. Callender wondered how he had missed it, then wondered if she knew more about the jungle than she had admitted. She might know more about the Thugs as well, and in fact, she might be leading him into a trap. Still, he followed her gently swaying back as she made her way through a stand of bamboo.

On the other side of it was a glistening pool of clear water.

''No crocodiles in that,'' said Callender, more disturbed than he cared to admit by this improbably opportune discovery.

''And it is a way to escape the heat,'' Sarala said. ''Perhaps we should stay here for the night. It will be dark before much time has passed, and this is a better place than many.''

Callender surveyed the area with a skeptical eye. A natural clearing surrounded the pond, and some large flat rocks offered relief from the hateful dampness of the ground. Mangoes grew nearby, and Callender noticed some wildflowers that he could not identify. It might have been an idyllic setting for a man and a woman alone, but only if they could forget the heat and the danger lurking everywhere.

''This looks like the sort of place where animals might come to drink,'' he said.

''There might be animals anywhere.''

''Well, at least Hawke's horse can have a drink, poor fellow.''

"Can he wait, please, just until I have a bath?"

"I forgot for a moment that you are a Brahmin. Go ahead. We won't dirty the water. I'll wait here with the horse."

Callender tactfully led the horse away and tethered it to a tree, conscious that it not only needed a drink but might well respond to the presence of the pool by walking into it. Rubbing his raw, perspiring neck, Callender reflected that he wouldn't mind being there himself, especially with Sarala. Although he made at least a halfhearted effort to be discreet, he could not entirely resist the temptation to watch the woman out of the corner of his eye, and he was at once disappointed and relieved to see that she behaved as he had observed the women of Calcutta doing when they walked down the steps called ghats into the Hooghly and bathed fully clothed. Yet Sarala was beautiful in the water, her long black hair now clean and smooth and straight, her face cool and content, the white silk of her sari clinging to her supple figure. He wanted to kiss her as he watched in the twilight, but a woman who would not share a coconut with him could hardly be expected to welcome the touch of his lips on hers.

And yet, having decided all this, he felt himself irresistibly drawn toward the pool. He looked down at her, and the steady, frank gaze that she returned to him left him utterly baffled, so different was it from the maidenly coyness or the roguish leers which were the expressions he had learned to read among the two classes of women who inhabited London. He could not take his eyes off her; he felt as if he had been hypnotized. The sheen of the sunset on her golden skin made her look like some pagan deity, and what he felt for her was less like lust than sheer idolatry.

A crash came from the undergrowth behind him, and

as he whirled to face it something black flew through the air toward the tethered stallion. Callender grabbed for his pistol and pulled the trigger again and again, but after the first wild shot, the gun issued only a series of clicking sounds. It was empty.

The panther landed on the chestnut's back, its fangs deep in the side of its prey's throat, so that when the horse toppled over, there was no danger from the thrashing hooves. Callender had never heard a horse make a sound like that before. The two animals struggled together for a moment, and then the black panther began to feed. Callender threw his revolver at it but missed again.

He turned toward Sarala and saw her standing quite still in the middle of the pool, the water up to her waist. "Stay there!" he whispered to her. "They don't like water." He was not as sure of this as he wanted to be.

At the sound of his voice the panther raised its head, and in the last of the light he could see that its black muzzle was stained red. Its eyes were cold fires reflecting the dying rays of the sun. It growled quietly.

Callender estimated that the animal was thirty feet away from him, a distance that it could undoubtedly cover in a few seconds. He longed to ask Sarala how sure she was that panthers stayed shy of men, but he was afraid of the sound of his own voice. He did not want to disturb their visitor at its meal. He wanted to run, but since he had told Sarala to stay where she was, it hardly seemed like a gallant gesture. Instead he lowered himself down onto a rock, as slowly and carefully as if it had been manufactured of spun glass.

After that, there was nothing to do but sit and watch as the panther burrowed into the horse's stomach and pulled out its intestines. Callender was not entirely unhappy when it became too dark for him to see.

The moon was a white sliver in the sky, and Sarala was bathed in its glow, but the panther was invisible in shadows as black as its hide. Callender knew it was there, however, from the sounds of ripping flesh and cracking bones. He wondered how long it had been since either he or Sarala had moved. He was developing a cramp in his left leg. Insects crawled on him with impunity, and inwardly he cursed the woman for the fastidiousness that had kept him out of the pool. On top of everything else, he was still unbearably hot.

Yet that did not prevent a chill from running through him when he heard something moving through the trees, and realized that it was not the panther. A figure stepped into the clearing. The panther hissed, and snarled, and gave a grating roar, but then turned suddenly silent. Callender thought that he could hear it moving toward the black shape of the man, and then there came a low rumbling sound which he could only describe as purring.

He felt as though he had been struck in the stomach with a cannonball. He did not need to wait until the man stepped into the moonlight, with the great cat at his side rubbing against him like a pet. Before he saw the dead face he was shouting at the sky: "Newcastle!"

Months of torment pushed Callender to his feet and sent him lurching across the rocks. He would have gladly died for the chance to touch his enemy with his bare hands, but the roar of the panther stopped him when fear of the vampire could not.

"Mr. Callender," Sebastian said. "I confess that I did not expect to find you here."

Callender staggered backward and fell against the rocks. He risked a glance at Sarala and was transfixed by what he beheld. Her sari trailed beside her on the water, and she was dressed only in her necklaces, her bracelets, and

123

her rings. She walked from the pool, her back straight and her head high, directly toward the panther and Sebastian Newcastle.

There was more at work here than Callender could comprehend. To see the beauty he had come to covet laid bare before the monster he despised drove him into a frenzy he was helpless to express. Sarala, both lush and lean, was like the carvings he had seen since he had come to India, and Newcastle like one of the native demons. The beast beside them as she walked into the dead man's arms might have been an emblem on the ornamental frieze that had come to life before him.

And as the moonlight carved shadows in the figures set before him, the scene began to change. Sarala, her sari still hanging from one hand, began to tear at Newcastle's clothes, while he writhed and twisted like a thing possessed. Callender could not tell if the panther or Newcastle was the one giving vent to those uncanny growls.

Stripped to the waist, Newcastle dropped to his knees, his white back heaving and darkening as malignant growths sprouted from his shoulder blades and bloomed into gigantic, leathery wings. Sarala clutched their clothing to her breast as the vampire embraced her, his great wings rippling like sails in a high wind, and suddenly they were aloft, dwindling in an instant to a black bat against the moon.

Then they were gone. Reeling, Callender stood halfway up again, but the merest murmur from the panther stopped him in his tracks. His mind was in such turmoil that he had no way of judging how much time elapsed before the animal turned tail and disappeared into the forest.

As if released from a spell, Callender leaped to his feet and screamed again that hated name. He searched through the underbrush until he found the pistol; it was empty, and bullets meant nothing to Sebastian Newcastle in any case, but Callender swore that his hate was strong enough to fill the gun and make it kill even the unkillable.

He cried again into the night: "Newcastle!"

And this time his cry was answered.

He heard a high voice calling somewhere to his right, a voice desperate with panic, and the word it wailed over and over was "Sebastian!"

Callender plunged into the trees, thoughts of a stricken Sarala filling his mind. Thorns ripped at his face and hands, tree trunks smashed into his shoulders, and vines sent him sprawling into the muddy ground, but still he ran, until at last he reached another clearing where he discovered a small boy in a breechcloth and a turban who sat in the grass and wept.

Callender pulled Jamini upright and then knocked him down again. "What do you know of Sebastian Newcastle?" he demanded.

Jamini, who had wandered lost for hours since he had escaped from Kali's shrine, was determined that if he could not find his master he would surely not betray him. He took a terrible beating from the Englishman, whose questions he hardly understood, and in the instant before a blow to the head turned his world black, he was glad to be relieved of further interrogation.

Callender was terrified at the thought that he might have killed the boy, his only link in India to the monster he sought. He sat and cradled the unconscious child throughout the steaming night, drifting between sleep and delirium until the sun burned his eyes open.

There was another distraction as well. Lieutenant Christopher Hawke and four Sikhs rode up with the dawn.

"You've cost me a horse and a night's sleep," drawled Hawke. "What was it, a tiger?"

125

"Panther," was all Callender could offer in reply.

"That was a damned good horse," said Hawke testily. "You weren't hard to track, but I can't say this excursion has endeared you to me, friend of my youth." His monocle gleamed.

Callender tottered somewhere between relief and despair. "I saw him," he said. "I saw Sebastian Newcastle. He's here. He's here, but he flew away."

"No doubt," said Hawke. "What's this you're holding?"

"He knows something," said Callender.

"Well, it appears there may be some power in this Hindu magic, after all. You've taken a handsome woman and transformed her into this wretched boy. Perhaps he is more to your taste?"

*T E N*

# *The Serpents*

Sarala sat in darkness. She knew nothing of the time; she did not even know if it was day or night. And she remembered very little of how she had come to be in this black room with its low ceiling. A sliver of dim light descended from somewhere up above, but she could not identify its source, although she had no difficulty in recognizing the gleaming figure on which it fell. Kali was the only thing she could see in the murky chamber, and even in feeling her way around, Sarala found only two other objects within its walls. One was a stairway to nowhere, its topmost step flush against a surface of smooth stone, and the other was an oblong box resting on the floor in the opposite corner. Neither of them struck her as reassuring.

Yet for some reason she was not really afraid. As she looked back over her life, which now seemed somehow blurred and unimportant, like last year's dream, she realized for the first time that she had rarely been alone before, and that those who had kept her company had also kept control over her. To her parents she had been a possession and plaything, and then a pawn in a scheme to unite their family with another for the enrichment of both. To her husband, a man she never chose but a man who had paid well for her, she had been a servant, and a hostess, and a whore. To his family, after he died, she had been a burden to be destroyed in a time-honored ritual, and to the British she had been a prisoner to be rescued and imprisoned and then rescued again.

None of it made as much sense to her as the peace of this cool dark place where she was alone with her thoughts at last. She tried to remember how she had come to be there, but all that filled her mind was a jumble of images: a pool of water, a wild beast, a man with a white face whose clothes and hair and eyes were black. Had she really flown through the night sky? If so, then she had been at another's mercy once again, and yet she felt with a conviction she had never known before that she had gone where she wanted to go, and that inside this prison of stone she was at long last free.

She dimly recalled standing naked before the stranger, naked as the statue of Kali was, and while she could not understand what had possessed her to display herself in such a fashion, for some reason she was not ashamed. The casting off of her garment seemed like the rejection of her past, of an existence where she could only scheme and brood and seethe with resentment at the invisible bonds that held her in place. Now another kind of life seemed to have opened before her, and with it the possibility of power. Yet she was dressed again in her sari of white silk, and her sense of something more to come was only a memory. She did not even know where she was.

She knew only that she was alone, and so it followed that the noise she heard could not be real. A small, stealthy sound, like the creaking of hinges in need of oil, had emanated from the dark corner where the long box lay, and Sarala held her breath while listening for it to come again. There was nothing, except for what might have been the rustling of cloth but was almost certainly imagination.

Then a voice called her name.

"Sarala," it whispered, and she felt as if a spider had crawled up the back of her neck. "Sarala," it whispered once again, and then she knew whose voice it was.

"You are the one who brought me here," she said.

"And you are the one who wished to come."

"I think I did, and yet I cannot tell you why."

"There is a mystery in it."

"I cannot see you. I cannot see anything but Kali. What place is this?"

"We are in a hidden room, below a forgotten shrine to Kali. Have you never heard of it?"

"Is this where the Thugs meet?" asked Sarala.

"Then you do know this place, Sarala. You did not tell the man called Callender about it?"

"I tell the English only what I wish them to believe," she said. "But why have the Thugs brought me here?"

"Perhaps it is not the Thugs who want you here. Perhaps it is the goddess."

"And you, the one who keeps his face hidden in the dark, what do you want?"

"You will see my face soon enough. And perhaps you will also see what I see. Do you believe that lives follow along a path that cannot change, that destinies are written somewhere, long before they are fulfilled?"

"That is karma," answered Sarala. "It is truth."

"Then you know why you are here."

"And was it karma that carried me on its wings?"

"No fate controls me, Sarala, because my life was over years ago."

"I am like one of the dead, too."

"But you are not like me, Sarala. Not yet."

The voice in the dark was interrupted by a harsher sound, as stone scraped against stone above the golden statue of Kali. The sliver of light in the ceiling was transformed into an open square of glimmering firelight, and its ruddy glow illuminated the face Sarala had expected, pale and scarred and shrouded in long hair that was blacker than the shadows.

"Stand in the corner," the stranger from her dream whispered urgently. "It will be better if they do not see you at once."

As she followed his advice she watched him hurry toward the stairs, then mount them and raise his hand to grasp the torch that had been thrust into their sanctuary. "Kalidas Sen," she heard him say. "Where is the boy? If you have hurt him, things will not go well with you."

"The boy?" gasped Kalidas Sen as Sebastian rose into the great vaulted chamber of the shrine. "We thought he was with you. He followed you last night. Don't you know where he is?"

Sebastian made no reply. Instead he was staring past the silk merchant toward the throng of men who followed him, fully twice as many as had appeared before. All of them were armed, and their weapons included knives and swords of shining steel, and also spears and bows and arrows made of wood. There were dozens of these, and he could not take his eyes off them.

"What is this?" Sebastian roared. "Have your men come to murder me?" His shape seemed to shift in the torchlight, elongating as it faded to a gray that matched the walls, his shadow rearing up to touch the topmost curve of the arched ceiling overhead. For a breathtaking moment there was only shadow where Sebastian had stood, then even that was gone, with only a few wisps of fog to take its place.

"Lay down your arms!" commanded Kalidas Sen, and those few of his men who had not already dropped their weapons did as they were told. "We only meant to obey you," the leader of the Thugs cried out, glancing around the shrine and even up above, as if he half expected to find Sebastian hovering there. "We brought you our old instruments of war so you could change them into guns!"

His followers, their hands empty, were backing toward the door, the voices joined in a murmur of dismay. One of them turned to make his exit and then let out a piercing scream. Sebastian stood before him, a black figure guarding the doorway.

"You have nothing to fear from me," Sebastian said, "as long as you serve Kali. She is the goddess of death, and I have come from the dead to be with you."

The men retreated to the center of the echoing, empty room, many of them huddled behind their leader as if they expected to be saved from the stranger who had shown that he was more than just a man. "We few have been faithful to the goddess," Kalidas Sen told them, "and see what she has sent us in return! Here is proof of her power, proof that you have all been wise to heed my instructions. We shall continue to plunder and murder, my brothers, for our own enrichment and for the glory of Kali, and now her emissary will stand at my side!"

"But what does he want of us?" asked a voice from the crowd.

"Much," Sebastian replied. "Is it enough for you to waylay your countrymen and empty their pockets? Do you imagine that the goddess asks no more of you? Are you men of such small vision?''

Kalidas Sen opened his mouth to reply, but then thought better of it. His men looked at him expectantly, and his face flushed as he realized that he was being questioned in two quarters at once. ''But this is what we have always done,'' he sputtered. ''This has been the way of Thuggee for centuries!''

''And what has it brought you?'' Sebastian demanded. ''A handful of silver and the hatred of everyone in India, where men are happy to believe that Thuggee is no more, and where even the priests prefer to hide the dark side of Kali from those who worship her. It is not enough for you to wage war on humble travelers when there is an enemy abroad in the land, an enemy that has defied Kali and reduced Thuggee from a vast company to this little band that shrinks even from my words.''

''You mean the English,'' whispered Kalidas Sen.

''Why should you kill anyone else when it is the English who rule India? Do you think it pleases the goddess to see her children bow before these foreigners? Do you think she will return to you in all her glory unless you rise up and drive them out?''

A murmur of dismay ran through the men. ''Drive them out?'' echoed their leader. ''It is impossible.''

''It may be impossible today,'' Sebastian said, ''but it may not be impossible tomorrow. The sacred rumel will twist around an English throat as well as any other, and when their leaders fall, the English will taste fear. And will not the heart of India rejoice to see the interlopers die? Soon every Thug could be a hero instead of a pariah, and our ranks would swell. Even the Moslems have tasted the sacred sugar, just as the Hindus have, and they could rise with you under the banner of Kali. Your kings and princes care only for their small domains, squabbling among themselves while the English Queen rules over all of them. They care nothing for their subjects, but Kali does, and slowly but certainly she can unite all India and set it free. Would you be the warriors to follow her in this, or are you content to steal the rings from dead men's fingers?''

Kalidas Sen was not prepared to answer this question. He could see that his men had been affected by Sebastian's words, and in fact, he had been touched as well, but the years had blessed him with prudence rather than boldness. To lead a few men and get a little gold was glory enough for him; he had no wish to see the world turned upside down. And he could not forget seeing his father hanged. "These are fine words," he said, "but what of the Army?''

"The Army could become our greatest strength in time, for the English have been imprudent enough to arm the men who will become their enemies. There are only a few foreign officers to control a horde of your countrymen, and when they revolt, all India will be ours!''

"He talks like he is one of us," muttered a Thug, "but he is an Englishman himself.''

"No," Sebastian answered. "I am nothing. I am only part of the endless void where Kali rules, and where all men will someday be her subjects whether they are cowards or not.''

"He seeks to rule not only us but India," someone said.

"It is Kali who will rule," Sebastian replied.

The time had come for Kalidas Sen to intervene. "My men have questions, as you see, and this is only right, for they knew nothing of all this until you spoke. Even I, who have led them for years, did not understand that you and the goddess expected such great things of us. You must forgive them if they want time to think on this.''

Sebastian remained silent.

"There are even some of them," continued Kalidas Sen, "who wish to put your magic to a further test, and that is why so many have come here tonight."

Sebastian's dark eyes gazed at the silk merchant, who turned away before he spoke again. "That can wait," he said, "but we must get below at once and take these weapons with us. There is always a chance that someone will pass by this spot, and we must not be discovered."

Sebastian stared at the pile of spears and arrows on the floor. It seemed improbable that the people of this land knew how dangerous a wooden shaft could be to him, but on the other hand no knowledge would be required to strike a fatal blow. Anything might happen, but the silk merchant's advice had its own merit, and in any case it would be disastrous to show fear to the men who might become the first followers of a new cult. "Very well," Sebastian said. "Bring your arms below. They will be destroyed when there are guns to take their place."

He led the way down into the earth, aware that there would be more to explain in just a moment, as soon as the Thugs discovered Sarala. "Will you use magic to turn these swords into muskets?" asked Kalidas Sen.

"No need for magic when there is gold," Sebastian said.

"You talk as if gold was easy to find."

"There is more gold in the world than there is freedom. And what you have in this room would be enough to equip an army."

"You mean the statue of Kali? That must never be touched! Just suggesting it is blasphemy! We will give up much for the goddess, but not the goddess herself!"

"It is only a statue."

"You mean to mock me! You think I do not know . . ."

The voice of the silk merchant was choked off by what

the torchlight showed him, and several seconds passed before he could speak again. A woman stood beside the golden goddess, and he recognized her face. "Sarala Ghosh! How did she come to be here?"

"She came with me," Sebastian said.

"You brought her here? You say you have been sent to lead us, but you will destroy us all! Do you know who this is?"

"I know who she will be."

"She will be the end of everything! She must die at once!"

Sebastian took his stand before the statue of Kali, on guard between Sarala and the Thugs. "You will not touch her," he declared. "She is mine."

Kalidas Sen noticed one of his men slowly raising a sword. "Put that down!" he shouted. "Put all the weapons down. I will take care of this!"

He stepped forward slowly, his empty hands outstretched, his words dripping honey. "You don't understand," he told Sebastian. "You can have the woman. Take her blood if it pleases you, but do it now. She must not live. She is a spy."

"And you are a fool, Kalidas Sen," the woman hissed. "Is there to be no end to this?"

"You see how she insults me?" asked the silk merchant. "She is our enemy. Why did you bring her here?"

"Kali commanded it," Sebastian said. "She spoke to me last night, after she had provided me with blood to drink."

"If Kali sent this woman to us, it is so she can be destroyed. Where did you find her? Was she alone?"

"She was in a pool not far from here, and there was a man with her."

"An Englishman?"

Sebastian nodded.

135

"But he was not one of them," protested Sarala. "He saved me from a pig of a man called Lieutenant Hawke, who killed Ramjoy Ghosh with the cannonball and would have done the same to me."

The mention of this death that damned the soul did not please the leader of the Thugs. "They would have done the same to you unless you turned informer, and you try to quiet us with a story about an Englishman who rescued you. Why would he do such a thing?"

Sarala hesitated. "I think he is mad."

"His name is Reginald Callender," Sebastian said, "and he cares nothing for Thuggee. He has come from England in pursuit of me."

"Then you should have killed him," said Kalidas Sen.

"It seemed ungrateful after he had brought the woman, but I do not think he will live long. He did not look at home in the jungle."

"I tell you this is one of their English tricks," insisted Kalidas Sen. "This woman has already brought them close to us, and my men will never follow you unless they see her die."

"It seems," Sebastian said, "that they cannot follow both of us." He was watching Kalidas Sen closely and was puzzled to see the ghost of a smile pass across his rival's lips. "Do you dare to defy me?"

"I have witnessed your magic," said the chief of the Thugs. "Now let me show you mine."

"No," whispered Sarala.

"You think these men are easily swayed, but they are not. I mentioned a test to you before, to show which of us is truly Kali's chosen one. You say you have conquered death, but you must prove it, as I have." Kalidas Sen turned toward his followers. "Bring forth my friends."

Although it would have been simple enough for Sebastian to kill the silk merchant at once, he realized such an action might not sit well with the men he hoped to lead. Instead he waited, Sarala trembling behind him, while two Thugs carried a large round basket forward and placed it at the foot of the golden goddess. They held it gingerly, as if they feared it might explode, and then stepped back from it with uncommon haste.

The basket rested on the ground, and Sarala stared at it so intently that she almost thought she saw it move.

Kalidas Sen sat down cross-legged in front of the basket and raised its lid. His men scattered to the corners of the subterranean chamber; some of them even crept up the stairs to put more distance between themselves and whatever their leader was about to reveal. Sarala thought of stories from her childhood, about uncanny things that hid in bottles. She watched the man on the floor put one hand into the basket.

Kalidas Sen twitched as if something had taken hold of him, then smiled as he withdrew his arm.

Wrapped around it was a cobra, its fangs embedded in his flesh, its brown scales undulating in the firelight.

Sarala screamed even before Kalidas Sen rose up and overturned his basket, sending a rain of serpents down on the statue, and Sebastian, and her. "Will Kali save you from this?" she heard the silk merchant shout.

One of the cobras fell directly onto Sebastian's face and hung there, its fangs pumping poison into his cheek, its long body thrashing glints of green and copper. He grasped it in both hands as Sarala retreated into Kali's golden arms, three snakes at her feet. Their heads were raised and their hoods were spread. One of them struck at her, its head snapping forward, but Sarala managed to step aside, only to lose her balance as a gout of blood splashed into her eyes. Sebastian had torn the cobra from his cheek and then

137

ripped it in half. He staggered toward Kalidas Sen as Sarala crashed down, her head falling only inches away from a strange albino serpent with scales as white as death, eyes as red as fire.

Half unconscious from her fall, Sarala's only thought was to keep still, but as she stared at the rubies gleaming in that narrow white head, she saw a hand thrust the creature toward her and felt the fangs cut like knives into her throat. Venom burned in her jugular vein.

Sebastian dropped to his knees and batted Kalidas Sen away with a sweep of his arm. He groped toward Sarala as another snake lashed out and bit his arm. He crushed it against the statue and howled with rage as he crawled forward like some wounded animal, his whole body on fire with pain.

Sarala could not feel her legs. Her mouth gaped open, saliva dribbling down her chin. Her tongue was paralyzed. Sebastian's face hovered over her, his features dark and swollen. She could not speak, and she could hardly breathe, but her heart was racing as if it meant to break out of her breast. That was the only thing she could feel except for the agony in her throat. Dimly she saw the white serpent flash before her eyes again, its ropy length twisting in Sebastian's hands, its scales stretching and splitting into chunks of bloody meat. Then Sebastian was upon her, his kiss upon her throat, a cool sweetness pouring through her body as she sank down into death.

The silk merchant struggled to his feet. Swaying slightly, his head light, he looked around the room. He was standing, but Sebastian Newcastle and Sarala Ghosh were not. "You see?" he said to his men. "It was a trick of the English."

Three of his cobras were dead, including the beautiful albino he had treasured most of all. He gathered up the four that were still alive and slipped them back into the basket with a mother's tenderness, taking care to avoid their glistening white fangs. He had been bitten twice as it was and felt giddy already, but he could not let the visions overwhelm him yet.

"It is safe now," he mumbled through numb lips as he covered the basket, not quite sure if he was talking to his snakes or to his men. As he stumbled forward on unsteady feet, the intoxication of the cobra bites exaggerated his senses until his steps resounded in his ears like the beating of a gigantic drum. He put his hand on Sarala's breast and waited for the heartbeat he was sure would never come. Her face was not as beautiful as it had been before. "Dead," he announced.

He turned Sebastian over with his foot. "Dead too. He always swore he was." Speech was becoming increasingly difficult for Kalidas Sen; the room shimmered around him. He would have to be left alone with his dreams soon. Almost as an afterthought he noticed the blood upon Sebastian's blackened lips. He had bitten the woman as they lay dying. There was something remarkable in that, but the silk merchant was past caring what it might be. Everything around him was vanishing into a golden light.

"Take them out and bury them with your picks," said the chief of the Thugs. "Then leave me alone with the goddess. She has chosen the one you must follow."

He endured the sounds of their departure like a hero undergoing torture, and when silence finally enveloped him, he sank down into his dream. The room with its walls and floor and ceiling disappeared, the shrine itself melted away, and the silk merchant was alone on a sea of gold with a goddess to keep him company, a goddess who was no longer made of gold. Her flesh was warm and supple.

Kali smiled at him.

139

## ELEVEN

# The Man with the Monocle

Lieutenant Christopher Hawke was bored by the regimental ball. There were too few women to act as dancing partners, fewer still who were pretty, and hardly any who were unattached. And those rare ones who were single, who had sailed from England and earned themselves the title of "The Fishing Fleet," intended to hook themselves something more promising than a young lieutenant with no money, no reputation, and no apparent prospects. Hawke had danced with two of them, as indifferent to their conversation as they seemed to be to his, and then devoted the rest of his evening to sipping brandy and gulping champagne. His mind was on prisoners, not dancing partners.

At midnight he strode across the expanse of waxed canvas that served the 5th Fusiliers as a dance floor, beckoned to a servant, and stepped out into the night. The waltz the orchestra was playing faded away behind him, its music melding gradually with a chorus of frogs from the nearby swamps. Even at this late hour the air was thick with steaming heat, and Hawke was glad for the chance to loosen the stiff black collar of his scarlet tunic. Sick of white trousers and gold braid, more than a little dizzy from drink, Lieutenant Hawke set out for a different sort of entertainment, one that might bring him the glory that could make a regimental ball a much more promising affair.

His servant carried a lantern before him as a guard against snakes, and Hawke lit a cigar to keep at least the more sensitive insects at bay. He scanned the empty sky for clouds, offering a hopeless prayer for the start of the monsoon that would put an end to this accursed inferno. Perhaps his luck would change with the weather.

He headed not for his quarters, but for the guardhouse. He hadn't bothered to question Callender or the boy with him until now, reasoning that a day spent stewing in their cells might help to loosen their tongues. At least it might have calmed Callender down; Hawke had no doubt now that his old schoolmate was mad. The boy, whoever he was, might prove to be more useful. Hawke decided to talk to him first.

At the entrance to the military prison, Hawke exchanged salutes with the native sentry, then exchanged a few rupees for the keys. For a modest outlay, he had managed to keep the existence of these two prisoners a secret from the other officers, which would certainly be a worthwhile investment if it enabled him to uncover a nest of Thugs entirely on his own. Of course it was inevitable that he take a few of the native troops into his confidence, but they knew better than to cross him in anything. Blowing away Ramjoy Ghosh had paid off, if not in the way Hawke had anticipated.

The atmosphere inside the guardhouse hit him like a brick wall. Its confines were like a furnace, its stifling air thick with the odors of human degradation and despair. Hawke's head reeled for a moment, but he pulled himself together with the thought that the place must be even more unpleasant for those who were confined within its walls, with no hope of release except through him. And if they had somehow managed to get to sleep, a sudden jolt in the middle of the night just might make them more amenable to persuasion.

He unlocked the boy's cell and gestured to his servant to hold the lantern high. The boy lay curled up in a corner, his eyes closed and his mouth open. He looked tranquil enough to annoy Hawke, who waded through the muck on the cell floor in his highly polished boots and gave the sleeping boy a kick on the kneecap. He was fairly gentle about it; the boy stirred, then sat up suddenly and opened his eyes. Before he realized where he was he had uttered a single word: "Sebastian."

Hawke was surprised to hear it. Of course Callender might have put that thought in the little beggar's mind, but it didn't seem likely. Perhaps there really was such a man as Sebastian Newcastle, after all, although expecting to find him in league with Thugs was really too much to hope for. And what could this diminutive wretch with wide eyes be expected to know about it anyway? Hawke would have gladly traded two of him for Sarala Ghosh, especially now that a good lashing appeared to be in order.

"Where is Sarala Ghosh?" asked Hawke.

The boy just looked at him, and his bewilderment seemed genuine. Hawke determined to be reasonable. "Where did Callender find you?" he asked. The boy sat and stared.

"Stand up when you're spoken to!" rasped Hawke, but there was no reply. Hawke slapped the boy's right ear.

"Please, sir. He doesn't understand you."

Hawke looked over his shoulder at the servant with the lantern. "Did I ask for your advice?"

"He is just a poor boy, sir. No English, I think."

Hawke considered the point and reluctantly acknowledged its probability. He was in no condition to converse in some filthy heathen language. "Very well," he finally said. "You talk to him. And no tricks, or he won't be the only one to suffer. Tell him to stand up!"

After a few of those nonsense syllables Hawke had never bothered to master, the boy got to his feet.

"That's more like it. Ask him what he knows about a man called Sebastian Newcastle."

More jabbering followed from the servant, and Hawke thought he saw the boy's eyes grow even wider, but he did not open his mouth.

"I just heard him speak the name! Ask him again."

Jamini had never been confined before, and the idea of spending the rest of his life in this little dark room frightened him far more than this officer did, yet he never even considered saying anything about Sebastian.

"Well. Let's try something else. Ask him about Kali."

Jamini stared at the Englishman's monocle, trying to decide what purpose it might serve. He had heard of idols with jewels for eyes, but never a man with a piece of glass for one. He tried to think about that instead of the question, which sounded to him like a trick that might somehow reveal something about the demon he had sworn to serve. He decided to keep still.

"Ask him his own name, then. He must know that!"

By now Jamini was too suspicious to say anything. He suspected that he might be struck again, but he had grown accustomed to such treatment long ago. The English soldier's face, pressed up against his own, was flushed and covered with sweat. A drop of it slithered down his forehead and dripped over the round glass in his eye. Jamini watched it, fascinated.

"Say something, boy," the servant whispered to him. "Don't just stand there. Say anything!"

Jamini hesitated, then his lips moved.

"Well?" demanded Hawke. "What did he say?"

"Nothing, sir. Nothing important."

"I'll be the judge of that! What did he say?"

"He says, sir, I beg your pardon, he says why do you have a window for an eye?"

Hawke took Jamini by the shoulders and shook him. "Think you're funny, do you?" he roared at the uncomprehending boy. "Well, laugh at this!"

Hawke lifted up his right leg and brought the heel of his heavy boot down with all his weight on Jamini's bare left foot. He could feel the small bones in the instep shatter as he heard Jamini scream.

Jamini could hardly believe what had happened, but he knew that it was wrong. A beating might make sense, but crippling a boy was bad for both the servant and the master. He was about to tell the English officer about this error in tactics when he fell forward in a faint.

Hawke stepped out of the way of the toppling body and let it slap down on the wet floor. "Joke with me, will you? This is no joke, boy." He looked at the heap on the floor and then at the man with the lantern. "Get out," he said. "We've more to do."

If he had been completely sober, he might almost have been ashamed of himself. As it was, he merely walked down the corridor until he reached Reginald Callender's cell. For this visit he stationed his man outside and took the light inside himself.

Callender sat in the middle of the room, his arms wrapped around his knees. "I thought I heard a scream," he said.

"Lots of screams in a prison, Reggie. You should be used to that by now.

Callender reflected ruefully that not long ago, when he was lost in the jungle, he had longed for the dubious security of a cell, but he had not imagined one like this. He felt like a man in an oven, and thought almost affectionately of his cold quarters in a London madhouse. If his present situation was more desirable at all, it was only because he was closer to Sebastian Newcastle.

"I've heard of the Black Hole of Calcutta," Callender said, "but I thought that was a torture that only these damned Hindus would inflict on a white man."

"It does get a bit sultry this time of year, doesn't it? And I think it was in June, just like it is now, that all those people died from being locked up in that room for a day, but of course you're not so crowded here. In fact, you've got a private room, old fellow."

Callender was strongly tempted to go for his tormentor's throat, just for the pleasure of inflicting even the most fleeting pain, but he managed to restrain himself. There was too much at stake for him to act like a lunatic. "Listen to me, Hawke," he said. "You don't want to keep me locked up here. What good will it do?"

"I don't know," drawled Hawke. "But it feels good. I like it."

Callender gritted his teeth when he heard his own words thrown back in his face, and he dug his fingernails into his legs to stop himself from lashing out. "I'm sorry," he said. "I shouldn't have mocked you like that, but I had to

145

get the woman away from you. It looked like you were going to kill her.''

"Well, I hope you passed a pleasant evening with her, because now you can see what it cost you.''

"It wasn't like that, Hawke!" Callender took a deep breath of fetid air. "All right, maybe it was. I wanted her, and not in pieces. But there was something more. It's as if I knew, as if a voice had whispered in my ear, that if I got her away she'd lead me to Newcastle. And she did!''

"And then he flew away with her.''

Callender sighed. "All right. Say that isn't true. Say I'd had too much sun. But I saw him, only a few miles from here. You can't keep me locked up now when he's so close. You can't let him get away from me! In God's name, Hawke, you can't let him get away!''

"And then this boy came walking through the jungle calling his name, is that it?''

"I swear to God it's true. If I could just talk to the boy . . .''

"I've tried it,'' said Hawke, wiping the sweat off his forehead with a gold-braided sleeve. "I broke his foot for him, and he still wouldn't talk.''

Callender longed to leap to his feet, but he only hugged his knees and rocked in the filth on the floor. "You haven't got him in a cell like this, have you? You'll kill him, Hawke! You can't do that. You've got to let me talk to him!''

"You should worry about yourself instead of him. You won't last much longer in here either, unless the rains come soon.''

"Oh, I won't die,'' said Callender. "Not yet. Not till I find Newcastle.''

His prisoner's assurance troubled Hawke. "Look here,'' he said. "You're a confounded nuisance. You kicked me.

You stole my gun. You got a damned fine horse killed. And for what? Why should I care if you find this chap Newcastle?''

"It's the Thugs, I tell you. He's in with the Thugs."

"There's no evidence of that at all."

"There will be after I talk to the boy. Please, Hawke. I beg you."

"Well, it won't do any good, but I suppose there's no real harm in it. And I'll be listening outside the door, just in case you do find out anything."

"Get me some water first," said Callender.

"I beg your pardon? Giving orders again?"

"I'm sorry, Hawke. I swear I'm sorry. Please let me have a little water. It's not for me, it's for the boy."

"I'll send my man for it. You'll need him anyway. Interpreter. The little beggar only speaks wog."

"Oh, Christ," groaned Callender. "I never thought of that. And I hit him so many times. Is he badly hurt?"

"Well, he's alive."

"What if I'd killed him?" Callender asked himself. "Was there ever such a fool?" He banged his head with his fist in a manner that made Hawke quite uncomfortable.

"He's not dead," Hawke insisted. "He's not dead. Look here, Reggie, can you stand up?" Callender tried, but might not have succeeded without a helping hand. "I think we can spare a little water for you too," Hawke said. To his considerable surprise, he found himself continuing to offer his support as Callender shuffled out of his cell.

A minute later Callender was kneeling by Jamini with a jug of water in his hand. He could hear its contents splashing, feel the delicious weight in his hands, but an almost superstitious dread prevented him from touching a drop before he had offered some to the boy who lay unconscious beside him. He poured a little on Jamini's face,

147

then repeated the process when he saw the boy's lips twitch. The dark eyes fluttered open.

What Jamini saw in the glow of the lantern was a face very different from the one with the monocle. This face seemed to be mostly hair the color of dried grass, which hung in a tangle over the forehead and sprouted from the cheeks and chin. The eyes were full of pale fire, but there seemed to be some sympathy in them. Jamini remembered those eyes when they had been angrier.

The stranger offered him a drink and said something he could not understand. Then a voice like an echo from somewhere in the cell said, "Do you remember me?"

Jamini nodded and took another drink with the stranger's help. "I'm the one who hit you yesterday," said Callender, and the interpreter told Jamini what he meant.

"I shouldn't have done that," whispered Callender, trying to communicate with the tone of his voice. "I'm sorry. Will you forgive me?" Hawke's servant hesitated over this. "Say it!" Callender told him.

Jamini nodded in answer to the question when it came, but he was so bewildered that the pain in his foot was almost forgotten. Nobody had ever apologized to him before, much less an Englishman. He liked the feeling.

Callender moved the lantern and looked down. "How's your foot?" He turned away immediately. What he saw was swollen, bloody, and shapeless, with a white gleam of bone protruding from it.

"That man with the glass eye killed it," Jamini said.

"And I killed him," Callender replied.

Hawke's servant was dismayed. "No, sir. I cannot say that."

Callender tried to keep his voice mellow. "You follow orders or I'll have you in front of a cannon."

Callender's message was dutifully delivered after this

148

exchange, and Jamini's face broke into a grin. "You killed him," he said. "Just like Sebastian."

"That's right," said Callender, "just like Sebastian. We're friends, Sebastian and I."

"What about that other man, the one by the door?"

"He's our friend too," said Callender. "He helped me kill the man with the glass eye. Now we can all escape together and go see Sebastian. But we don't know where he is. Do you?"

Jamini was suddenly silent. He wanted to be back with Sebastian more than he had ever wanted anything, but he needed more proof before he could trust this stranger. "If you killed that man, show me his body."

"I can't. We threw it in the river."

Jamini thought a little longer. "If you're Sebastian's friend, tell me a secret about him."

"Oh, that's easy." Callender was smiling. "I know all his secrets. How he turns into fog, and flies through the night, and sleeps through the day. I even know what he drinks. But I don't know where he's hiding now."

"I promised to protect him. How can I be sure you don't want to hurt him?"

"But how could I hurt him?" asked Callender, his voice a soothing whisper. "How could anyone hurt him? He has too much magic. It's his friends I'm worried about. The ones who are with him."

"The Thugs? They are not his friends."

"No," said Callender, his heart racing. "They're not really his friends, not like you and me. But he uses them, doesn't he? He makes them do things?"

Jamini nodded.

"That's right," said Callender. "And these English soldiers want to kill the Thugs, so we have to warn Sebastian. But we don't know where he is."

"But you were almost there when you found me."

"That's right, I was. But I couldn't quite find the place."

"It's pointed on top," Jamini said. "It's made of stone. And hidden under it is a beautiful statue of Kali with no clothes on."

"That's right," said Callender as the voices of the boy and his interpreter blended together in a dark duet. "I had forgotten, but that's right."

Something turned sick in Callender's soul, but he had found Sebastian Newcastle.

# TWELVE

# The Avatar

When Kalidas Sen returned to the shrine on the afternoon after his serpents had done their work against the enemies of Kali, he was accompanied by a man driving an ox cart. Rattling on its rough bed were a dozen wooden kegs. They had cost the silk merchant dearly, but he had decided the expense was necessary if he wished to reassert his authority over his bewildered band of Thugs. After they had unloaded the cart he sent it and his companion back to the city; this way there would be no attention attracted to the shrine, and its contents might appear to have arrived by some sort of miracle.

There was time for Kalidas Sen to shift the small barrels into the secret room where the golden goddess stood, for it was no longer haunted by the presence of the pale man with the dark eyes, and no one could forbid him to enter before nightfall. When he finished, he sat sweating and gasping on the steps of the shrine, hoping for the breath

151

of a breeze that never came. He watched the sun sink into a bank of purple clouds and prayed to Kali that they would bring rain. Then he retreated into the comparative coolness of the underground chamber to wait for his men.

They arrived as they always did, slipping through the darkness alone or in small groups, keeping to the shelter of the trees, making no sound, leaving no trail. Their black clothing had been the silk merchant's idea; after the British had exposed the old practice of Thuggee, travelers would no longer grant hospitality to strangers, and so his men had changed from deceivers into predators, like the black panthers that skulked through the jungle. It was a band of shadows that worshiped the goddess of death.

Not until all his men were finally gathered together did Kalidas Sen lead them below. Rarely had he seen so large a group assembled at one time; frequently one or another of them found himself too busy with his business or his family to attend, but tonight there was not a single Thug missing. Fear was painted on each face, and curiosity too: everyone had heard of the wonders performed here, and no one knew what they meant. At last Kalidas Sen arose and spoke.

"You all know," he began, "that some of my beautiful cobras have been destroyed. This saddens me, but it was a necessary sacrifice in the service of Kali. Many such offerings must be made to the goddess, and to thoughtless men she appears to be a cruel mistress. Yet we who are initiates understand that for everything we give her, we receive much more. Kali grants us wealth and power, and also the greatest gift of all: the promise that she will be our guide and comfort after death brings us to her domain. For a blessing such as this, no sacrifice is too great."

He paused to let his words sink in and then continued. "You all know that among the devout there are those who have willingly cut off their own fingers to please Kali. Of course this is not a suitable sacrifice for we who wield the sacred handkerchief.'' He smiled at his followers, and a few of them realized that he had made a joke. ''There are even those,'' he went on, ''who have cut off their own heads, or so we are told, and this is not an easy thing to do.'' He smiled again, this time more broadly, and several of his men laughed nervously.

''But Kali is generous, and all that we lose in her service will be replaced. Just today, my brothers, I traveled through the jungle as you did, to visit this shrine, and on my way I saw a cobra sunning itself on a flat rock on the right-hand side of the path. This was a good omen, and I gathered him up, but as I traveled farther I found another serpent on the left-hand side of the path! This too I gathered to me, brothers, and felt myself doubly blessed, but when I drew near to this shrine, I found before me, curled upon the steps, a great white cobra, of such a size as I have never seen before! And here they are, all of them, gifts of the goddess!''

Kalidas Sen opened his basket and emptied it out on the floor, so his followers could see the truth of what he said. None of them would ever know how much he had paid in Calcutta for these snakes, or for the surprise that was still to come, but the gasps of amazement from his congregation assured the silk merchant that his money was well spent. After a suitable interval he gathered up his pets, treating them gently since this was not the time to let their poison intoxicate him once again.

''And so you see, my brothers,'' he continued, ''how Kali rewards us. We have made other sacrifices in recent days, and they have been more harsh than the loss of a few serpents. We have lost men, and we have lost one who came among us, surely sent by the goddess herself, to show us her power and guide us along the true path that turns neither to the right nor the left. Yet when you see what care she has shown in such a small thing as the serpents, can any of you doubt that everything will be restored to us, that we shall have all we have given her returned doubled and redoubled?''

A roar of approval came from a dozen throats, and Kalidas Sen basked in it. He had a very ordinary face, not one that would be noticed in a crowd, and he was of ordinary height, but as he spoke his features took on a glow that seemed to dignify them, and he even appeared to grow taller as he raised his hands in a gesture of exhortation. It was almost as if the magic that had been Sebastian's was somehow transferred to him.

"Let me speak further of the one who has come and gone,'' he said solemnly as the crowd subsided, "for there can be no doubt that he was a true avatar of the goddess herself, a part of her vast spirit incarnate in human form. Now he has returned to the bosom of Mother Kali, but his last act, which many of you witnessed, was to sacrifice himself to save us. You saw how he let the cobras bite him, caring nothing for himself as long as he could sink his own teeth into the throat of Sarala Ghosh, the informer who would have betrayed us. He brought her among us so that we could see her destroyed, and only her would he allow his fangs to touch, for he was brother to the serpents, and his poison is such that the woman will burn with it throughout eternity. When such a one is sent to protect us, can there be any doubt how much the goddess loves her Thugs?''

A few of those present might have doubted if their leader had told the story with perfect accuracy, yet even they were swept away by the idea of such divine justice, and again the subterranean room rang with their cheers.

"But there is more!" shouted Kalidas Sen. "One such as he was sees far into the future, and what he said about rising against the British may well come to pass. It is a vision, and its fulfillment depends entirely on you, for each man that you recruit to our cause brings us closer to the day when we shall be strong enough to rise up and rule all of India. And to that end, behold the gift that Kali's avatar has left for you!"

With a dramatic gesture he pulled aside the cloth that covered his treasures. "Kegs of gunpowder!" he crowed. "Not one, but a dozen of them! Fuel for the weapons that Kali will send next, fuel for the fire that will sweep across our land and set it free!" From his men's awestruck faces, he judged that he had achieved the desired effect. It might be weeks before they realized that the powder was nothing without the means to use it, and by then the dream would have faded and events would be under his control again. He folded his arms across his chest, gazed on his followers, and smiled. To sway men in this manner was almost as good as robbing them.

Far above Kalidas Sen, above the vaulted roof of the forgotten shrine, above the night birds that soared through the purple sky, the clouds that had drifted from the west swelled to the bursting point. The months of stifling heat had created their own antidote, and the monsoon was at hand.

At first the rain fell gently, the rare drop splashing on a green leaf, an animal's back, or the stones of Kali's shrine. The distant rumble of thunder was inaudible to those who hid under those stones, and so was the increasing vigor of the downpour, which now danced and rattled like tiny gunshots on the figures of maidens and monkeys that decorated the hiding place of the golden goddess. A flicker of lightning turned the night to day, and it roused creatures sleeping in the jungle.

Now the shower turned to a cloudburst, the water slashing downward in impenetrable sheets. The marshy ground of the jungle absorbed all it could hold in a matter of minutes, and then its lowest areas of land transformed themselves magically into shallow lakes, their surfaces rippling with the rain as if they were bubbling with life.

And from one of these little lakes a human hand emerged, its pale fingers groping toward the sky like the tendrils of a plant in search of nourishment. A face floated up beside it, plastered with wet black hair that obscured all of its features but an open, hungry mouth. Sloping shoulders hunched out of the water, and in the ghastly glare of the next lightning bolt the figure of a man emerged, his lean body encrusted with mud, small stones, and crawling creatures of the earth. His broad back bent, he felt beneath the surface of the water as if there were something he had lost in its depths.

White silk twisted in his hands, its coating of earth boiling away in the torrents of rain, and suddenly a woman was in his arms.

"The venom of a snake is nothing compared to mine," Sebastian said. He and Sarala turned their streaming faces toward the shrine.

Within its walls, Kalidas Sen experienced the slight sense of loss that all performers feel when their moment of triumph passes and ordinary life begins again. He alone knew that the cobras and the gunpowder were no more than shabby tricks to maintain discipline, so he alone knew that sorcery had vanished from the cult. He wondered what to tell his men now, and he longed for another miracle to prove to them that they were more than common thieves. However great a threat to the silk merchant's power had been posed by the man called Sebastian, he had nevertheless represented a true manifestation of the unknown, like the ghouls Kalidas Sen had seen when he was a boy. And like those ghouls, Sebastian would haunt his dreams.

The leader of the Thugs let out a sigh. "There is no more, my brothers," he announced. "Go home and think on all of this." The Thugs milled around the golden statue of Kali, examining the kegs of powder while keeping well away from the basket of cobras. Somehow they seemed reluctant to depart. Clearly they were not in a defiant mood, but Kalidas Sen could tolerate not even the slightest disobedience at this point in his career. Mounting the steps and opening the passage, he commanded them to follow with a sweep of his torch.

"There is no more to see tonight," he said. "Go home." He peered into the gap the sliding stone had made, and then he began to behave in a most unusual manner. While his baffled followers looked on, Kalidas Sen came slowly down the stairs again, taking one step at a time and walking backward, his eyes never turning from the square of darkness at the top. He dropped his torch, and one of the Thugs, suddenly conscious of the gunpowder, snatched it up again with a startled cry.

Kalidas Sen stood rigid at the bottom of the stairs and stared upward as Sebastian appeared on the topmost step. The Thugs responded to their visitor with a silence that showed more fear than any sound they might have made. They shuffled toward the rear of the underground chamber and their leader gravitated toward them, until dozens of men were pressed against the wall that was most distant from the man they knew was dead. Some of them had buried him.

And yet Sebastian, however dead they knew he was, glided down the stone steps toward them, his black clothing and his black hair dripping with every step he took, his black eyes empty and awesome.

Kalidas Sen, to his credit, was the first of the Thugs to recover his senses. "Rain," he said. "He's been in the rain. The monsoon has come. And see what else has come, my brothers!"

His rhetoric now was like a runaway horse that not even Kalidas Sen himself could hope to stop. Inspired by panic, his voice echoed through the room, and he was as astonished to hear it as any of his men. "Now you see," he shouted, "that everything I told you was true and more than true! Even I did not dare to tell you what I knew, what the goddess had promised me, but now you see with your own eyes that Kali's avatar has returned to you!"

Sebastian waited at the foot of the stairs, neither moving nor speaking, as if he had decided to hold himself in check until the silk merchant's speech came to an end. And Kalidas Sen could not keep still. "The goddess gives more than she receives, and even death is no barrier to her. Each sacrifice will be rewarded, as I told you, and the one who gave his life to punish the wrongdoer is restored! All praise be to Kali!"

"All praise be to Kali," echoed Sebastian, and Sarala entered the room.

Kalidas Sen lost his voice, and then his knees failed him as well. He sank down on the stones as the woman in white approached.

"This man lies," Sebastian said, "and he is accursed in the sight of Kali."

The silk merchant fell forward so that his forehead rested on the floor. His shoulders shook, and his feet drummed uncontrollably on the damp rock.

"The rest of you come forward," Sebastian said, "and gaze upon the true incarnation of Kali."

As if drawn by invisible wires, the Thugs stepped past their fallen leader to crowd around Sebastian and Sarala. The woman was still beautiful, her body outlined by clinging wet silk, and her eyes were now as dark and distant as her companion's. "Both of us have endured death for you," Sebastian told the men, "and both of us have been transformed by it. Now you will serve this woman as you would serve the goddess, and you will obey me as you once obeyed Kalidas Sen. Together, we shall lead you in the conquest of this great land, a conquest that will require a sacrifice of blood. Much will be spilled, but it will be good in the eyes of Kali, for it will be the blood of those who have invaded and corrupted her domain. India is her treasure, and the British will not relinquish it willingly, but with the help of the goddess we shall prevail!"

The Thugs looked at one another, confused by a multitude of changes, and certain only that miracles could not be denied. "It will take more than gunpowder to bring us to our goal," Sebastian continued, "and more than blood. It will take brave men. And in token of that, each one of you will leave some of his blood behind tonight." He picked up one of the bowls that held the offerings to Kali. "Which of you will be first?"

A man stepped forward at once. "You shall be doubly blessed," Sebastian said, then led him to the statue of Kali and cut his right arm on her golden sword. A spoonful of bright blood trickled down into the bowl, and Sarala moved toward it. "Take your rumel," Sebastian told the Thug, "and use it to bind up the wound. Let each man do the same, and let the bloody handkerchief become the emblem of our new order. Let each man who has made his offering depart, but return here before midnight tomorrow, for there will be more for you to learn."

The Thugs crowded around the golden goddess, most

of them eager to perform the new ritual now that they knew how little harm there seemed to be in it. "Is there any here who would deny this gift to the goddess?" asked Sebastian. No one protested, and each man stood in line to make his offering.

"And what of the silk merchant?" asked Sebastian. "Will he be one of us, or will he die?" Several of the men looked back to see what the response would be, and one of them let out a gasp as he pointed to an empty spot on the floor. The crumpled figure of Kalidas Sen was gone.

"He has crept away like the jackal that he is," Sebastian said, "and he has chosen the death from which there shall be no awakening. If any of you see him before I do, make certain that he does not live. He will not dare to inform on us, for it would cost him everything, but such a coward and deceiver shall not live to cast dishonor on Thuggee."

One by one the men stepped forward to meet the golden blade, and one by one they slipped out into the storm. The bowl was almost overflowing by the time the last man left, and Sarala drank from it eagerly. "There will be more soon," Sebastian promised her. "There will be rivers of blood."

Outside, in the jungle, Kalidas Sen ran blindly through the deluge. He had been robbed of his fortune and his honor, and in the eyes of his own men he was no more than a whipped cur. He was like a child again, helpless and afraid in the presence of the supernatural; but like the child he had been, Kalidas Sen swore to himself that he would use what frightened him against his enemies. Sebastian and Sarala might be dead, but he knew something that even the dead feared.

# *T H I R T E E N*

# *The Monsoon*

"Then there are Thugs near Calcutta, after all," admitted Lieutenant Hawke. "Either that, or the boy is as mad as you are."

Reginald Callender only sat and glared at him.

"We'll have the cannon along, I think," said Hawke. "The twenty-four pounder."

"You're crazier than I am," Callender snapped. "You can't drag a gun like that through the jungle. It must weigh more than a ton."

"Quite a bit more, actually, but that won't bother us. After all, we're British, old fellow, and we're here to show these wogs what we can do. Why do you suppose God gave us oxen? Or elephants, if it comes to that?"

"Oh, fine! Come crashing through the jungle like a brass band, and still hope to surprise the enemy?"

"There's a way," Hawke murmured thoughtfully, "there's a way."

161

"And while you try to find it, almost a day has passed. We should have attacked them at sunrise!"

"These things take time, Reggie. It's not the easiest thing to organize a campaign like this one, especially in secret."

"Tomorrow morning, then."

"Oh, no, old man. Tomorrow night."

Callender was out of his chair and halfway across the room before Hawke got his hand on his revolver. "I said tomorrow night," insisted Hawke. "And do me the kindness to keep your seat, or I'll have to put your legs in irons, too."

Callender returned to his wicker chair. He stared at the iron manacles around his wrists and the heavy chain between them, then looked up at the punkah revolving lazily overhead. "He'll be awake if the attack comes at night."

Hawke took a pinch of snuff, drawing it up into his nose with a ferocity that was matched by the sneeze that followed. "I don't give a damn about this man Newcastle," he told Callender for what seemed like the hundredth time since last night. "The boy said the Thugs met after dark, so after dark is when we'll attack. I hope that's quite clear now, because you're becoming a bit of a bore on the subject, and I'd hate to have to put you back into that cell after all you've done to help me. It's so hot there, you know, not that it's much better here."

After the jungle and the guardhouse, Hawke's quarters looked like paradise to his guest, who nonetheless decided not to mention that fact for fear that it might supply his capricious host with another opportunity to torment him. Instead he glanced around the sitting room to distract himself, and something caught his eye that he had paid no attention to before: on one whitewashed wall hung a pair of hog spears, used in hunting wild boars for sport. Cal-

162

lender's chain clanked as he gestured toward the long wooden shafts with their sharp iron tips. "You'd be smarter to bring one of those than a cannon."

"Of course," Hawke answered irritably. "Just the thing for knocking down stone walls."

"Still, that's what I'd bring."

"Really? And what makes you think you'll be coming along?"

"But you promised!" sputtered Callender. "You said that if I got the boy to talk . . ."

"I said no such thing, and you know it. Didn't have to. You were dying to talk to the boy. Positively dying!" Hawke was smiling, but he was also fingering his gun.

Callender decided to drop the subject for a moment, even if it took all the willpower he possessed. Showing Hawke that you wanted something seemed to be the surest way to guarantee you wouldn't get it. Instead he held up his hands. "I wouldn't have much of a show anyway, wearing these."

Hawke only grunted, but Callender thought there was a glimmer in his eye.

"You did promise to have a doctor look after the boy," Callender said quietly.

"Did I? I really don't remember."

"That foot of his looked to me like it might get infected."

"He's only a little savage, after all. What does it matter?"

"It doesn't matter, really. But I thought the word of a British officer still did."

Hawke raised an eyebrow; it was not the one that held his monocle in place. He played with his waxed blond mustache for a moment, then went to his writing desk and scribbled a hasty note. "Boy!" he shouted. "Punkah boy!"

The big fan in the ceiling stopped, and a few seconds later one of Hawke's servants rushed in. "Take this to the doctor right away," said Hawke, and then he turned to Callender. "I'm afraid we'll have to do without the breeze for a little while, but that little beggar's comfort is worth much more than ours, don't you agree?"

Callender inclined his head, his conscience at least partly mollified. The thought of the boy disturbed him more than he wanted to admit. "I suppose the doctor will have him taken out of the guardhouse, don't you think? The heat can't be good for him."

"I've given specific orders that he should stay where he is, and you'll be joining him if you don't shut your mouth." Hawke consulted a map spread out on the table in the center of the room. "If we go north on the river," he said to himself, "we can get above the spot where they meet, and there won't be any chance of running into them on their way in from the city. Yes. That should work."

"And you can carry the cannon in a rowboat," suggested Callender.

"Shut up, Reggie. I'll have that sent by land, and I'll arrange for it to arrive precisely at midnight. It's only a few miles to this old temple anyway. We'll be in position by an hour after dark, keeping an eye on things, and if there's any reason for it, we can strike at once. Otherwise we'll wait for the big gun and let them have it at midnight. Anything wrong with that?"

"You're not allowing for Newcastle."

"Forget about Newcastle! Damn Newcastle to hell!" Lieutenant Hawke poured himself a brandy and looked out his window at the sunset. He would have sworn he felt something like a breeze from outside, but of course that could only be imagination. "Look here, Reggie. Let's go over this one more time. I know you think this Newcastle is some sort of a wizard, but that's one of your what-do-you-call-'ems. Delusions. There's no such thing. And there's nothing to this Hindu magic either. I know some of the old hands around here talk about it like it's real, but that just means they've gone soft from too much sun. All we have here is a flock of wog bandits and a renegade white man who's thrown in with them. And all we have to do is shoot the lot of them, except for a few prisoners we'll need to put on display."

"But you can't shoot him! And you can't capture him either!"

"No, that's right. He'd fly away." Hawke gulped back his drink. "I'm awfully sorry, Reggie, really I am, but I think it's time you were back in your nice, warm cell. Would you like a drink first? A cigar?"

"But you can't send me back," protested Callender.

"I most certainly can."

"But we were at school together!"

"And what does that have to do with anything?"

"I lent you a shilling once, so you could buy candy," said Callender reproachfully.

"It was a sixpence," Hawke snapped back at once.

"What difference does that make? We were friends!"

"Just because we were both at Eton at the same time, it doesn't mean that I'm your friend, you know."

"But think of all we've been through together, Christopher. You don't mind if I call you Christopher, do you?"

"I'd rather you didn't," Hawke answered stiffly.

"Just as you say, of course. But you might at least take these handcuffs off . . . "

"Why should I? Last time you were free, you kicked me!"

165

"I know I did," admitted Callender. "It was the woman made me do it, really. Something about her I just couldn't resist."

"She was a damned fine-looking woman, wasn't she? And that's another reason why the manacles stay on." Hawke picked up the brandy bottle once again, but this time he poured two drinks.

Callender looked at his with some suspicion, then decided he was better off with a glass in his hand than he would be expiring from thirst back in the guardhouse. He took a small sip, and then another. "I wonder what's become of her," he said.

"You said she went off with that man, didn't you?"

"That was days ago. He might have killed her by now. He does things like that, you know."

"All the more reason for you to hate him, isn't it?"

"But if she isn't really dead, she'll be in that old temple with the Thugs. And you're going to send your men in there with guns."

"I wouldn't let that worry you too much. No man of mine will take a shot at anyone who looks like she does."

"They might not realize who she is," said Callender. "Especially in the dark."

"Then she'll have to take her chances, won't she?"

"But it's not her fault she's there!"

"I couldn't say about that. You told me yourself that she took off her clothes and ran into his arms. Isn't that right?"

"She had no choice, I tell you. He was controlling her somehow. He must have been!"

"Ah, yes. More magic. Well, I'll wager that a well-placed cannonball will put an end to that."

Callender sat forward in his chair. "What was that?" he whispered.

166

"I said I'll wager that . . ."

"Be still! I thought I heard something. It sounded like gunfire."

Lieutenant Hawke listened, and then he swore. He rushed to the window and thrust his head out. He looked up at the darkening sky as the distant sound echoed across the arsenal. Callender stood up to follow him. "You sit down or I'll knock you down," said Hawke. "That isn't gunfire, you fool. It's thunder!"

Hawke threw his brandy glass across the room and watched it shatter against the opposite wall. "Damn!" he shouted. "It's going to rain. You were right, Callender. We should have launched our attack at once. We could never have been ready so fast, of course. But of all the times for it to start raining!"

Callender could only stare at Hawke and wonder. "It'll stop before long, won't it? Why, there's been no rain at all since I've been here."

"There will be now, and it won't stop for months. This isn't just rain. It's the monsoon!"

A flicker of lightning turned the room pale blue for an instant, and thunder cracked as though the sky had shattered.

"Monsoon," repeated Callender. "I've heard of that."

"You've heard of it," sneered Hawke. "By God, it's a good thing I've got you under guard. You shouldn't be allowed to go out in the world."

"It's only rain, isn't it?"

"More like old Noah's flood. It's damned near impossible to fight in weather like this."

Finally Callender began to understand. "But you've got to fight! You can't let him get away! Not after all I've done . . ."

Hawke grasped him by the throat and shook him the

way a storm shakes a tree. "You haven't done anything!" Hawke shrieked at him, his red face only inches away. "I'm the one who did it all. Me! I found that handkerchief, and I arrested the woman, and I'm the one who captured that wretched boy you're so worried about! I'm the one who'll catch the Thugs, and I'm the one who'll get the glory! And you've done nothing but get in the way and make up fairy tales!"

He let Callender drop back into his chair and examined his own trembling hands. "Of course I admit it's a coincidence that the man you're looking for got in with the Thugs, but that's all it is, just a coincidence."

"You're wrong," said Callender as he rubbed his throat. "Not even this rain is an accident."

"I suppose you think Sebastian Newcastle started it? By God, that's the last straw. You're coming on this little expedition with me, rain or no, and I'll show you that there's no sorcery out there. He's just a man, Callender, and tomorrow night he'll be a dead one!"

For once Callender resisted the temptation to keep talking. Somehow he had said the words that would make him part of the assault on Kali's shrine, and that was as much as he could hope to accomplish. Hawke was calling for his guards.

"After this change in the climate you won't find your cell quite so uncomfortable," Hawke said, "and at least you'll be out of my way. Come on, Callender. We'll stop off to visit your little friend before we lock you up for the night."

Two of Hawke's Sikhs, their shoulders spotted with raindrops, entered his bungalow and pulled Callender out of his chair. They remembered him from the afternoon by the river, and they did not treat him gently.

Outside, the rain fell steadily, its sound like the hissing

of a thousand snakes, and despite his companions Callender enjoyed himself. He was soaked to the skin, but for the first time in weeks he was wet with water instead of perspiration.

"It may be pleasant for the first few minutes," Hawke told him, "but you'll soon find the change in the weather is just another kind of hell. Now everything in India turns green, and then it rots."

Callender ignored him.

"At least you're getting a wash," continued Hawke. "Your clothes were becoming a trifle ripe, to tell you the truth, but I suppose they're good enough for where you're going."

The intensity of the downpour increased even in the few minutes it took to walk across the parade ground, and by the time the four men reached the guardhouse, it was coming down in torrents. Bathed in an eerie light, all of Dum Dum seemed to be covered in rippling gray glass.

Lightning shattered the image, and in that moment Callender was ushered into the guardhouse once again. The clean smell of the storm gave way to the odor of hopelessness with which Callender was all too familiar. Rough hands pushed him down the dark corridor.

"Stop for a minute," Hawke told his men. "We're going to pay a call on a sick friend." He jingled the keys he held in front of Callender's nose, then smiled and used them to open a cell door.

The only light inside came from a narrow slit in the thick wall; it showed Jamini sitting on the floor and staring out into the storm. His left foot was wrapped in something white.

"There you are, Callender. All nicely bandaged up. No doubt he'll be as good as new by the time he's hanged."

Jamini twisted his head around at the sound of Hawke's

voice. His mouth dropped open; then he began to speak rapidly in Bengali.

"What's he babbling about?" Hawke asked his men.

"Crazy boy. He says you are a dead man, sir."

"What? Oh, yes, that's what you told him, isn't it, Reggie?" Hawke pulled Callender forward so the boy could look at him, then gave instructions to the Sikh.

"Tell him this man is a liar. He's not Sebastian Newcastle's friend, any more than I'm a dead man. Tell the boy he was tricked. He told us where his friend was hiding, and it will be his fault when we kill his friend tomorrow night."

The message was repeated, and Jamini's face was such a picture of dismay that Hawke burst out laughing as he slammed the door.

"For God's sake, Hawke," Callender began. "There's no need to torture the boy . . ."

"Oh, shut up, Reggie. It's only a bit of fun. And it'll give the two of you something to think about during the night, won't it? Have a pleasant rest."

Hawke sauntered out into the rain with a jaunty wave of his hand, leaving Callender and the keys with the two Sikhs, who took this opportunity to show the prisoner just how they felt about being forced to throw their weapons into the waters of the Hooghly.

They had a gift for expressing themselves.

# FOURTEEN

# The Ghoul

The storm that battered Calcutta was a mere echo of the one raging inside Kalidas Sen. He wandered in the jungle throughout a long night which sent even the beasts in search of shelter, for his spirit now was wilder than theirs would ever be. Animals do not know shame, nor do they plot revenge.

By morning he had collapsed under a tree, and the tempest had also spent some of its force, subsiding into a steady downpour that would continue without significant interruption for many weeks to come. A sane man would have certainly gone home, but the silk merchant was no longer sane, and he no longer had a home. He was certain that Thugs were waiting for him in the city with their rumels ready, and equally certain that others were searching the jungle in the hope of finding him, but he was finally too exhausted to go on, and in any case he had nowhere to go. He took a lesson from the rain and settled down, realizing that he would need all of his strength for what he planned to do when the next night fell. Eventually he slept.

And while he slept he dreamed. He dreamed of water as a man sleeping in a puddle should, but the water he dreamed of was the river that flowed nearby, the great Hooghly that stemmed from the sacred Ganges. He dreamed of what lay at the bottom of the great river, of the thousands of corpses that Calcutta had buried there and he dreamed of what fed upon them in the darkness.

And when he woke, he knew where he would find what he needed. He had already known what it would cost him.

He spent most of the afternoon gathering his courage for the sacrifice to come, and only when he had convinced himself that the sun behind the clouds was setting did he move west toward the river. He would have liked to act sooner, despite all his fear of what was coming, but the thing he hoped to summon was a creature of the night as surely as Sebastian was, and it would not come before its time no matter what gifts he offered.

The surface of the Hooghly seethed and shimmered as fat drops splashed into it, but Kalidas Sen hardly noticed; his mind was on his fingers. The memory of his own words from the night before returned to mock him now; he had spoken of fanatics who cut off their own fingers, and he had even made a joke about them. Now he was about to follow their example.

The finger would be partly for Kali, for he still hoped in spite of everything that she had not abandoned him. He might have been a liar and a fraud at times, but he was also the one who had revived Thuggee when the world said it was dead. Perhaps the goddess would remember him for that. If not, the finger would have to be solely for the pleasure of the thing Kalidas Sen feared even more than the walking corpses in the shrine, the half-glimpsed hairless thing that had haunted him since childhood, the thing that rooted around a man's corpse like a pig. The thing that fed on dead men's flesh. The ghoul.

Kalidas Sen held up his left hand and let the rain fall on it. Suddenly it seemed a feeble thing, pathetic, yet all the more precious for that; he could hardly bear the thought of wounding it. He had decided hours ago to take the little finger of his left hand, since it was least useful and would be easiest to spare, but now all at once this struck him as unconscionably cruel, like hurting the weakest member of a family. Tears joined the raindrops running down his cheeks, and he had not even scratched himself yet.

Nonetheless, this was the finger he had chosen, and he knew that if he diverted his attention to another, it would soon be throbbing with a special tenderness as well. He reached for his knife, the one he had stolen from the weapons hidden at the bottom of the shrine. The blade was curved and tapered, thicker at its back than its front, broader at its base than its tip, and of course there was nothing remarkable in any of this, but somehow the knife fascinated him now, almost as much as his finger did. With its little wrinkles and its tiny hairs, and the white crescent at the bottom of the nail, his finger was a miracle.

He pressed it down on a wet rock and carved it off. He had to lean his weight on the knife, and he could feel the blade grinding against the bone as he searched for the joint. Some of the time he screamed.

When he was done, he wrapped his hand in his rumel. "Let the bloody handkerchief be our emblem," he told the absent Sebastian. Then he talked to Kali, and finally he sang to the river. Its water and the sky above were gray.

When he had no more to sing or say, Kalidas Sen sat in the mud with his legs crossed and looked at his finger on the rock. The rain beat down on his bowed head and turned the red stain on his handkerchief to a pale pink.

The rain roared like a fire. Something thick and glistening raised its head out of the river and heaved toward the shore. Water surged over the bank.

Either Kali or coincidence had answered the silk merchant's prayer, but in any case the ghoul had come. It crawled toward the finger on the rock, its slippery flesh wobbling, and Kalidas Sen was so intent on his revenge that he did not become violently sick until he smelled it.

The magic that gave Sebastian new life each evening was subtle rather than sudden. He did not spring into awareness of the world at the instant that the hills hid the last ray of sunshine; instead he drifted slowly upward from an abyss of dreams. The depths were coolly silver, as sweet as the golden light of day was hot and harsh, and the dreams and the day met when both were dark.

Images appeared before his sightless eyes; they were the faces of three who were missing and must be found. The first was the boy Jamini, who had run into the trees and disappeared. What had become of him? Sebastian had meant to seek him out and shelter him again, and yet he had done nothing of the kind. The shrine was hardly a safe refuge now, rather a home for vipers and lunatics and women who drank blood, but was it this thought that had led Sebastian to abandon the boy, or was there something else?

The second face belonged to Kalidas Sen, who had crept out of the shrine while Sebastian bled the Thugs. The treachery of the silk merchant should have been repaid with death at once, but somehow he had been spared, as if letting an enemy live was the most natural thing in the world. How could that have happened?

The third face was Reginald Callender's, and this one was the most remarkable of all. The man had come from halfway around the world, and just a glimpse of his expression was enough to show that he was bent on vengeance. In London he had seemed no more than a harmless fop, but something had changed Callender, and perhaps it had been the very contempt Sebastian had showered upon him. The man burned with a fever that made the leader of the Thugs look pale, and yet Sebastian had passed him by with no more than a greeting. Was such carelessness conceivable?

All three of them were in the jungle now, perhaps: two rabid animals and a helpless boy. Either of the men might have found Jamini and slaughtered him for spite; they might even have banded together to plot an assault on the shrine. Surely Sebastian had recognized all this before? What had he done last night?

He could hardly remember, but the face of Sarala swam into his dream. He had seen to it that she was fed, but there were hours afterward that he could not recall. In truth, though he was rising slowly from his own dark domain into the human realm, his memories of Sarala refused to coalesce. Only brief flashes remained, illuminated as they might have been by lightning bolts. A vision of Sarala had sent him racing from the shrine, although it meant abandoning the boy, and the sight of her nude body rising from the pool had made Callender seem no more than a shadowy figure fit to be ignored. And when Kalidas Sen could have provided a feast for two vampires, Sebastian had forgotten him to extract a little taste of blood from each assembled segment of Thuggee, and then he had let Sarala drain the bowl.

There was more in all this than the taking of a new mate, and there was more in it of giving than of taking.

Asleep in his wooden box, Sebastian could not find the rest the dead are promised.

Above him, in the passage which led to the hidden chamber of the shrine, something pale and puffy pushed against the stone. It was nearly phosphorescent, and it was almost a hand.

The rock rolled back at its touch, and a rubbery bulk squeezed through the opening. When it worked its heavy way down the dark stairs, it left a trail behind it like a slug. Yet in the shadows its shape suggested some forgotten ancestor of man.

Sebastian stirred. Sleep still held him in its silver net, and yet he was aware of movement in the shrine. He struggled to bring life to his frozen limbs as he heard the lid of his coffin rise.

What greeted him, however, was hardly an attack. The touch was so light, so delicate, that it was like the caress of a lover, reminding him at once of Sarala. Perhaps the blood of all those men had given her a greater strength than his, enabling her to rise before he could.

He continued to believe that it was Sarala who fondled him until blunt teeth ripped away a chunk of his left leg.

The searing pain gave him the strength that the twilight had not. Sebastian heaved himself up halfway out of his coffin, knocking the lid aside. It clattered to the floor as his hands lashed out at his assailant, catching it where its throat would have been.

The ghoul looked at Sebastian with idiot eyes. His fingers sank into its flesh without effect, and it lowered its head again to pull away the muscle of his calf.

The ghoul might have been made of jelly for all the impression Sebastian's fingers made on it. There was nothing to grip, only a mass of wet putrescence. By now there was little left below his knee but bone.

176

He had heard before of creatures who devoured the dead, and now one was consuming him. Could this be what it was like for mortals when a vampire fed on them? Was this greedy, empty thing his brother?

Sebastian twisted to one side and tumbled out of the coffin, landing on his back with the dripping, flabby ghoul on top of him, never relinquishing its grip. His pain and shock and sudden weakness made him helpless under its assault; he could no more have turned into a mist than he could have burst into flame. He could only fight it like a man.

He reached out for the coffin lid and, clutching it in both hands, brought it down again and again on the ghoul's head. For an instant he thought the first blow had some effect, but then he felt those heavy jaws take hold of his thigh, and he realized that the slab of wood had no more impact than an oar slapping against a wave.

The creature was as alien to Sebastian as a European vampire was to India, and he could not imagine how to vanquish it. Such slippery strength, combined with lack of substance, filled him with a horror that was more than fear of his own demise.

In desperation, he smashed the coffin lid against the wall, breaking it as he could not break the ghoul. There was an insane satisfaction in the violence of the act, and then an inspiration too. Clutched in his fingers was a jagged wooden stake. Might it be a weapon against this thing?

He raised the sharp shaft high and drove it down into the glistening, translucent back. The monster heaved and quivered under the impact, and Sebastian struck repeatedly, probing for its heart.

The ghoul raised its head, rubbery lips twisted in a stupid smile.

Sebastian struggled with the urge to curse or even

177

scream. His head fell back, and he saw the golden statue of Kali looming over him. The goddess was smiling too. He might have prayed to her for help if the thought had crossed his mind, but as it was he did no more than whisper her name between clenched teeth.

"Kali."

The goddess was still smiling, but now it appeared that she was leaning closer to him, as if she wanted to make sure she had heard what he said. Her face grew larger as it came nearer; all at once it was rushing toward him until it blotted out everything else.

A heavy, liquid thud reverberated through the room, and it was followed by a short, high-pitched squeal. The statue's head rested by Sebastian's own, and the attack on his leg had ceased.

Sebastian sat up. The golden statue had fallen facedown and he was half trapped beneath it, but it had crushed the ghoul, whose loathsome body was dissolving in a puddle of greasy fat that stank of bile and urine.

Sarala stood where the statue had been. "A monster such as this must be killed with one blow," she said. "A second blow brings it to life again."

"And Kali fought demons that would not die," Sebastian said.

Sarala stood in darkness, and Sebastian's head swam. But could his wounds alone explain the weakness he felt in her presence? Could the transformation into one of the living dead, which he had observed so many times before, explain the awesome power that seemed to flow from her in waves? Was it only a shadow that made her seem to have more arms than any woman should?

"What are you?" Sebastian demanded of her. "What have you become?"

## FIFTEEN

# *The Golden Goddess*

Outside, the rain plummeted down on the black stump that was Kali's ancient shrine. And inside, under the earth, Sebastian lay crippled at the feet of the being he had known as Sarala. He could hardly see her, but he heard her quiet voice.

"Who dares love misery and hug the form of death, to him the goddess comes."

"And is that why you have come to me?" Sebastian asked.

"Did you not call my name?"

"Then without that sign of homage you would have willingly seen me destroyed."

"You have been of use to me, whether you willed it or not, and so your call was answered, but it would have been better for you to be denied."

"Better to be devoured by that monstrosity?"

"Better to let endless suffering come to an end."

179

"And then what?"

"You of all men know, for it is what comes in your dreams, when the illusion of the universe dissolves. You hide from the light, for light is a veil that blinds those in this world to the beauty of eternal darkness, which is the final truth and the only liberty. Why will you not embrace it once and for all?"

Sebastian almost smiled at this. "And if there is such liberty, why have you abandoned it to take on this earthly form?"

"I am time itself, and always eager to destroy worlds."

"And for this you endure the pain of becoming flesh?"

"Where is it written that the gods shall not know pain?"

"Or those who are neither gods nor men," Sebastian said as he gazed down at the bare bone of his leg. "And what of the woman Sarala?"

"She has gained the only liberty that lasts. She is the chosen one, and thrice blessed. She is the one you wished to be."

"I wished to rule, not to be transformed into pure spirit."

"Then you do not know your own heart. Or else you lie even to Kali, and even after you sought to be her avatar. The kingdom you wanted is not to be found on the earth."

"Where is it, then?" Sebastian demanded. He tried to drag himself out from under the weight of the statue. Broken pieces of it lay on the floor, precious metal swimming in the slime remaining where the ghoul had died. He was covered in the vile liquid himself, and yet he was conversing with a deity.

"You must look higher," she told him, "or deeper. For freedom is not achieved by having power over others."

"And did Sarala want this freedom you have given her, or was she merely swept away to make room for you?"

"She wanted freedom more than anything, and in part it was her fury that transformed her. She has been possessed by others since the day she was born, and only in my possession of her is there finally liberty. Her family meant to kill her with a fire, and the British would have killed her with their gun, but it was left to the serpents to kill her, and for you to kill her once again, so that she could be born into my realm where there is neither life nor fear of death. And when men did not seek to murder her, they carried her off, whether she wished it or not. The soldiers saved her from the fire, and the man Callender saved her from the soldiers, and you saved her from him and from the serpents, but where was her will in all of this? Only now, when she is one with the darkness, is she finally out of men's power."

Sebastian considered this. "But if men had not done all these things to her, she might never have reached this place to undergo her transformation."

"She was destined to be here, chosen before time began. It is karma, and everything that you and all the others did, whatever you may think, was done only to bring the woman here so I could be reborn. What do you think drew you to India?"

"I know now," Sebastian said.

"You thought you would be king here, drive out the foreigners and rule in their place, but you are alien here yourself. This land is not your home."

"Nor is any other land," Sebastian said. "But Sarala will rule this one."

"She will not rule, for that is not my way. It is not glory or grandeur that I bring, but chaos and confusion. The woman will not be recognized for what she is, and few will see her as you do now, but she will spread the disorder that is the first step to wisdom."

"And when will she begin?"

"Soon enough. For Kali there is nothing but time."

"Then I have come here on a fool's errand," Sebastian said. He pushed against the statue, his effort fueled by anger and frustration, until slowly the golden goddess rose. And when the idol stood erect again, he stumbled back against a wall, his weight hardly supported by his crippled leg. "Must I exist like this?" he demanded. "My body racked to match my spirit?"

"If you choose to exist, you must endure. But you have been hurt before and yet grown whole again."

"Not without blood."

"Then seek blood, Sebastian, but you will never find it here. And if you leave this shrine, you will never return."

"Then you will prevent me?"

"Do you doubt that I can? Do you doubt that I can destroy the very stones?"

"And could you destroy Calcutta too?"

"It would be easier to destroy you, but I shall not, for there is magic in you, and you have given me this transformed body, one that feeds on death and yet will never die. I will not destroy you, but you will leave India."

"Banishment?" asked Sebastian.

"There is nothing for you here. I offer you the limitless joy of eternal night, and you tell me of your hunger. Go forth and satisfy it, then, for Kali has no more to offer you."

"And the others who helped to bring about this incarnation? What will their fates be?"

"You need not think of them again, for what will come of them has been ordained. Even as I see that you will journey on, I see what will become of the English soldier, and the silk merchant, and the boy."

"The boy?" echoed Sebastian. "What do you know of him?"

"All that I need to know. He will be mine."

"You will not make him a Thug!"

"The Thugs have served their purpose now, and they will vanish from the earth."

"Then what need do you have of Jamini?"

"You ask too many questions. What is the boy to you?"

"He was my friend," Sebastian said.

"Then be grateful, for soon you will be alone again."

Sebastian slumped against the wall. "Perhaps it is better so."

"There is one more, the man called Callender. This one's fortune is still bound up with yours, yet he is surely not your friend. Nonetheless, he will be with you until one of you is destroyed."

"Then I would be well advised to kill him when I can."

"Whichever one of you dies first will be the first to end his suffering."

"But he knows Sarala, and he is the only man in India who knows the powers I have, the ones I gave to her. I must stay here, to destroy him and defend her."

The voice of the goddess had been low and sweet, but now it rose into a roar. "Even if unbelievers should enter my temple, even if they should defile my images and rob me of this shell, what is that to you? Do you protect me? Or do I protect you?"

Her questions reverberated through the dark chamber, and so did the silence that followed them. Sebastian's only answer was to gaze at the foulness on the floor.

When he finally spoke, it was only to state the obvious. "Kali was created to destroy the enemies of gods and mortals both. She has no need of me."

"Look on my golden image and see the truth of what

you say. For it is there, and not in the face of this woman, that you will perceive my true countenance.''

Sebastian looked and saw a golden creature dancing with delight, a sword in one hand and a severed head in another. Yet fingers had been broken from the two hands which gestured toward him, and the once beautiful face was flattened and twisted and torn.

"All mortals lose their fear by having faith in you," Sebastian said, "for to embrace the void is to conquer fear. But Kali is not as beautiful as she once was."

"Then I have lost that much for you, Sebastian. Ask no more of me."

"A battle was never won without wounds," he remarked as he attempted once again to stand. The woman behind the statue was still hidden in the shadows, and he did not wish to see precisely what she had become, but when he took a step forward and crumpled to his knees, he heard a gasp of sympathy come from the darkness.

"Then the woman is still there," he said as he tried to rise, "and not only the goddess."

"We are one."

"I would bid you both a graceful farewell, but I find that I am too weak to transform myself, and too badly hurt to walk."

"Then you must crawl, Sebastian."

He dragged himself toward the stairs. "I am like an infant in your presence," he said with a touch of bitterness. "Or am I more like that monster you slaughtered for me? When I thought it would defeat me, I was more angry than afraid, but what did frighten me was that we seemed so much alike."

"As long as there is existence, there is fear."

"But am I like that scavenger?"

"Not if you climb upward."

184

Sebastian grasped at a step with both hands and pulled himself painfully toward the opening in the ceiling. His progress was slow and silent; minutes passed before he reached the top. His fingers found the balanced stone and pushed it open. Cool air drifted into his face, and with it came the sound of rain. He struggled toward it, then turned his head for the last time.

"Will I ever be free, goddess?"

"Only beyond form is perfect liberty. And only time is immortal."

"Then surely Kali will wait for me. And there is no need for me to make haste."

"I shall look for you, Sebastian."

As he slithered along the passage he heard the rock scrape shut behind him. The steady drumming of the rain in the jungle drew him onward across the barren floor of what had once been Kali's shrine. Like one of the silk merchant's snakes he made his way, and after a time he reached the door that led outside. A thousand drops of darkness greeted him.

He tumbled down the steps into the mud. From far away he heard the laughter of Kali, and as the sound touched him he somehow struggled to his feet.

He took his first shambling, crippled step.

## S I X T E E N

# *The Siege*

Only twenty-four hours after the onslaught of the monsoon, the people of Calcutta were beginning to suspect that the rain might be worse than the heat it replaced. Blinding walls of water dropped into the city, and the streets were flooded almost instantly, so that walking became more like wading.

The Hooghly River was rising, its waters simmering in the downpour, when a party of soldiers and one civilian boarded a dinghy and made their way upriver from Dum Dum. Native troops manned the oars, and in fact, the only English on board were their officer and his prisoner, a bruised and bloodied figure whose hands were manacled. Behind these two sat a pair of bearded Sikhs, upright and imperturbable in the face of rain that hurled down upon them like a flight of arrows.

This expedition to the north was unauthorized, but Lieutenant Christopher Hawke never doubted that he would receive retroactive approval from his colonel when he had uncovered a nest of Thugs. A bid for hero's status was certainly worth a few hours of inconvenience or even danger, although Hawke did not anticipate much in the way of risk. His men were handpicked, and the cannon coming by the overland route would breach the walls of any heathen temple he had ever seen. In fact, Hawke expected so little in the way of trouble that he had brought Callender along as a joke.

"Comfortable?" Hawke inquired.

"It's a bit damp for a pleasure trip," Callender replied.

The two men instinctively crouched down as if that could protect them from the rain; everything on the boat was soaked except for the muskets wrapped in oilcloth. Hawke's field uniform of heavy khaki had turned the color of river mud, and raindrops bounced on his helmet. His waxed mustache began to droop, and his fogged and streaked monocle served only to blind him. Anyone less conscious of his image would have taken it off, thought Callender, but clearly the idea never entered Hawke's head. Callender was past caring about his own appearance, but his face felt like a smashed banana and his bedraggled clothing had long ago ceased to be white.

When they had traveled far enough to convince him there was no time to turn back, Callender lifted up his head and turned to his tormentor. "You think you're making a fool of me, don't you, Hawke, dragging me along like this? What you don't realize is that I want to be here. You're taking me to Newcastle, and before long you'll see what he really is."

"Oh, I know what he is, old fellow."

"Do you?" sneered Callender.

"Well, you told me, didn't you? When you told me how

to kill him, I realized he must be a pig. And since you're not armed, I brought you this pig sticker!''

Hawke reached into an oilcloth bundle and pulled out one of his hog spears. He handed it to Callender and burst out laughing, loudly enough to attract the attention of his men.

Callender took the wooden shaft and held it as well as he could in his shackled hands. He looked at Hawke and smiled. "Very good of you," he said. "I might have better luck with it if you'd unchain me, though."

"Of course!" said Hawke. "That's only fair, isn't it? Now, where did I put that key?" He put his hand in one pocket, then in another. An unmistakable smirk began to spread across his face as he pantomimed a desperate search. "Damn!" he said. "I don't know what's happened to my memory. Really I don't. I'm afraid I forgot to bring the key."

Callender did not expend his energy on a reply. He clutched his spear and kept his eyes fixed on the turbulent black water of the Hooghly. The rain rattled down.

The day grew darker and Callender guessed that there was probably a sunset somewhere behind the gray clouds. Overcast skies, approaching night, and sheets of rain soon made it almost impossible for him to see anything except on those occasions when lightning threw the landscape into an instant of sharp relief. He silently cursed Hawke for insisting on a night attack; the siege on the shrine would be more like a game of blindman's buff.

Just when he had decided that the journey on the river would never end, one of the Sikhs said something to his companion, sparking off a conversation Callender could not understand. Instead he watched the two men, the same pair who had beaten him in the guardhouse. Their red turbans were drenched and dark, and water dripped from their full beards, but their eyes were still bright. After a minute they appeared to have come to an agreement.

"We stop here," one of them shouted over the downpour.

Hawke twisted his head around to look at them. "Are you sure of that?"

"Kali back that way," said the Sikh spokesman. "A short march."

Hawke grinned and turned to Callender. "We've passed that temple now, and we can creep up on it without much risk of running into any of those shifty beggars on their way here from Calcutta. Just a little more time now, and you'll be poking Newcastle with your stick there. Don't get too rough, though, will you? We'll have to take a few of them alive."

An order from one of the Sikhs brought the dinghy drifting slowly over to the right bank of the river; before it reached the shore most of the men jumped out and walked. Callender tried to follow suit, using his spear for support, and succeeded in maintaining his balance in the rushing water until Hawke came wading up behind him and clapped him on the back.

Callender stumbled and fell face-first into the muddy river. With his hands chained in front of him, he found it almost impossible to push himself up again, and for a moment he imagined that he was about to drown, but one of the Sikhs grabbed him by the collar and dragged him onto the comparatively dry ground. Choking and sputtering, he found himself confronted once again by a smiling Hawke.

"Slipped, did you? Well, it'll wash off soon enough."

While Callender realized that getting any wetter than he had been was impossible, he would nonetheless have murdered Hawke, no matter how swiftly the Sikhs exacted retribution, if not for his desire to reach Sebastian Newcastle. At that, Callender was starting to wonder which of the two he hated more.

He allowed himself to be pushed into the jungle by the Sikhs, all the while hugging to himself the thought that they were forcing him to go exactly where he wished to be. He tried to fight back against the more rational part of his mind, which insisted on reminding him that, under guard and manacled, he was about to face an opponent of uncanny power, one whose strength Hawke and his soldiers could not comprehend.

The dark journey through the jungle was a nightmare, with vines that tangled the feet, shrubs that ripped clothing, and branches that whipped at his face, but Callender was past caring about such things, and at least the trees afforded some shelter from the incessant, maddening rain. Sooner than he expected, they arrived at their destination. One of the Sikhs put a burly arm in front of him to block his way, then pointed to a black bulk dimly visible through the storm-tossed trees.

All Callender could see at first was a squat tower whose roof rose to a dull point, but then a brief flare of lightning gave him a glimpse of a glistening brown surface carved with the figures of men, women, and beasts. There was something else, too, something that made him blink and rub his eyes and look again. He prayed for another flash of lightning, and it came, illuminating a gaunt black form that hunched and limped away from the shrine as if it were a carving come to life.

"Newcastle!" he screamed, but a deafening blast of thunder drowned him out. At once the Sikhs were upon him. A heavy hand covered his mouth as he was dragged to the ground; a man's weight covered him, and he saw a knife gleaming in front of his face. He made one attempt to struggle, felt the blade nick his cheek, and then gave up.

"Would you like a gag to go with your chains?" Hawke whispered in his ear.

Callender shook his head. Hawke waited for a few seconds, then nodded to the man whose hand was smothering Callender. The knife stayed where it was while the hand pulled away, and Hawke put a cautionary finger to his lips.

"Did you see him?" croaked Callender. "That was Newcastle. He's getting away."

"That old cripple was Newcastle? It doesn't take much to scare you, does it?"

"You've got to stop him, Hawke. For God's sake . . ."

Hawke slapped him lightly on the side of his face that had been cut. It was no more than a love tap, but there was a world of meaning in it. "I told you I don't care about Newcastle. I only want the Thugs. Newcastle means nothing, and neither do you. I only brought you here to keep me amused."

The knife was less than an inch from Callender's eyes, and the Sikh who held it looked more than willing to diminish the distance. Callender felt tears coming, but told himself that they would be invisible as long as the rain fell. He wanted to argue, but no words would come.

"It just might be worth it, though," said Hawke, evidently talking to himself, "to find this superannuated lunatic you think is the devil himself, to see just what he is, and to show you. Where'd you meet him, in the madhouse?"

Callender smiled as stupidly as he could and nodded agreement.

"We have a while to wait before the cannon comes," Hawke observed after examining his pocket watch. He put his foot on Callender's chest and his hand on his revolver, then tapped each of the Sikhs on the shoulder and pointed out directions for them to take. "Find that man," he said.

Callender sighed and lay back in the mud. Water splashed in his face. The Sikhs hurried away into the trees.

Time passed slowly with nothing to do but wait. Hawke tapped his foot impatiently on Callender's collarbone. He produced a silver flask of brandy and took a sip of it. "Want some?" he asked. Callender shook his head.

"Keeping a clear head, are you? Very wise."

The minutes moved like mud. Hawke's troops huddled together under the trees, seeking a shelter that did not exist. The whole world was water.

A scream came tearing out of the jungle, a human voice expressing fear and agony. Everyone looked up, as if they expected to see something in the sky. Then silence settled over them again.

"That's the end of your Mr. Newcastle," said Hawke.

"I don't think so," said Callender. He smiled. Hawke did not.

Hawke looked at his watch. "Where are those Thugs? If that damned boy lied, I'll use his head for a cannonball."

"They may be too intelligent to come out on a night like this," suggested Callender, and his idea was rewarded with a kick.

"It's the only kind of night they'll see for months," said Hawke.

A second scream cut through the night, this one ending in a soprano gurgle that made Hawke's neck twitch.

"That wasn't Newcastle either, you know," said Callender. "I'll miss those two fellows. Such splendid beards."

Hawke was too distracted to respond. He turned toward his soldiers. They squatted in puddles, their eyes wide, and Hawke was just enough of an officer to realize that morale was poor. "Don't just sit there," he hissed at them. "Get those muskets loaded and ready. There's going to be a fight when the big gun comes."

He took his foot off Callender and swallowed more brandy. "He must have caught one of them," he muttered, "but the other one will be back soon with his head. Too bad, but it couldn't have been him screaming like that twice. You only die once."

"Newcastle can die as often as he likes," said Callender.

Hawke's Hindu soldiers had unwrapped their muskets and draped the pieces of oilcloth over their heads like an awning. He kept an eye on them as each one took up a smooth-bore musket, the weapon known familiarly to British troops around the world as "Brown Bess." He watched them working with their ramrods, and saw the activity was good for everyone except for Callender, who just stared at the shrine with a wild expectation in his eyes.

A distant glimmer lit up the sky, and Callender struggled to his feet. "Two of them," he whispered to Hawke. "They're coming."

Hawke whirled and peered into the downpour. He squinted at what might have been moving shapes in the darkness. "Are you sure? Don't play tricks on me, Reggie. It's worth your life."

"Didn't you see them? Look! They're going in."

A turbulent cloud kept Callender alive when it discharged its current in a jagged fork, brightening the night as two men scurried for the shelter of the shrine.

Hawke actually rubbed his hands together. "That's right, my beauties," he crooned to the Thugs. "Come on now, all of you." The Sikhs were forgotten in a minute.

They might have been good soldiers, but soldiers were born to be replaced. Thugs were invaluable.

Hawke began to pace back and forth with excitement, then stopped abruptly as if he realized he might attract attention despite the shelter of the trees. He kept his eyes on the stretch of open ground in front of Kali's shrine, but each time the sky lit up he glanced rapidly around at the terrain, seeking more substantial cover than the local vegetation could provide. Expecting the Thugs to launch a counterattack meant giving them more credit than they deserved, but there was no point in taking any unnecessary risks. A group of moss-covered rocks, some of them half as high as a man, looked like his best bet, and he was about to order his men toward them when he spotted three more pilgrims approaching the ancient structure.

"They would wear black," he said to himself. "Well, they'll have use for mourning clothes before too long." He was so keyed up that it was starting to worry him; he could feel his pulse throbbing in his head. Another Thug arrived, and then another. Hawke consulted his watch and saw that he still had almost an hour to midnight, the time when the cannon was scheduled to arrive. At this rate, the party coming through the jungle might arrive too soon and scare some of the Thugs away. He almost wished his reinforcements would be late, yet knew there was little hope of that with Sergeant Jarvis in command. The man had no imagination, but he was deucedly efficient.

Hawke tried to console himself with the thought that Thugs left at large might actually be to his benefit, provided he captured enough tonight to make a good show. He could build a career out of bringing these brown assassins to justice if he played his hand properly. Of course, having Callender around might prove to be a bit awkward, but this night's work might put an end to that problem, especially since Callender could hardly be expected to defend himself. And if he didn't have the decency to die, perhaps something could be arranged.

He watched Callender, who sat hunched forward with his arms wrapped around his knees, his sandy hair matted over his forehead. The man was actually rocking back and forth in the mud like some sort of idiot child, and Hawke felt a twinge of sympathy for him, which he put to rest with the thought that his old schoolmate would be better off dead.

Another pair of Thugs arrived, and then four more together. He was losing count in his excitement, but Hawke already had more than enough. "Keep those muskets covered up," he whispered to his soldiers, and one of them saluted smartly, just as if the order had not been carried out some time ago. "And don't kill them all. Five rupees for each one you take alive. Seven rupees."

By now the devotees of the goddess were arriving with almost dismaying frequency; Hawke realized that his unit was outnumbered by more than two to one and tried to console himself with the realization that the Thugs were not armed, unless they carried handkerchiefs. Still, he could not help thinking that the jungle was alive with these fanatics and that they were noted for creeping up behind their victims. Before long he was looking back into the trees more often than he was watching the seemingly endless stream of Thugs. He congratulated himself for thinking of the cannon.

He wanted to make a dash for the rocks, but didn't dare while so many of the enemy were passing nearby. He began to worry about Callender, who was now staring up into the clouds, apparently keeping an eye out for the man he said could fly. The lunatic might do something unforgivable at any time, Hawke told himself, like shouting out or running down to ask the Thugs where Newcastle had gone. So many men had passed by that Newcastle might have been among them, in fact, although Hawke had noticed no one with a limp. He took out his revolver, cocked it, and laid it beside Callender's head. "Just sit quietly," he said, and he noticed with dismay that the hand holding the pistol was trembling visibly.

And now the space before the shrine was deserted, an open area that impressed Hawke as somehow ominous. Had everyone arrived at the party, or was something else going on? The barrel of his gun shook against Callender's head. Minutes crept by and nothing happened. Rain fell.

All at once the ancient shrine seemed to spring into life. Lights flickered from the open entrance, and the echo of chanting seeped out into the night.

"They're singing," gasped Hawke. "Just like a church choir."

The chanting rose into the air, exotic, high-pitched harmonies that made Hawke's wet skin crawl. He saw the nervous glances exchanged by his Hindu soldiers but could not find the heart to chastise them. The music was unearthly, beautiful and horrible at the same time. And as it swelled up, a high, shrill keening at the fore, the light from the temple became a blinding white, something no torches or lanterns could have caused.

A wildly gesticulating figure leaped into the light, its shape silhouetted against the glare. Arms raised above its head, emitting piercing shrieks, it charged toward the trees where Hawke's men hid.

Hawke raised his revolver and pulled the trigger. Callender, half deafened by the sound of the shot, clapped his hand to his ear and howled. Their assailant advanced a few more staggering steps and dropped in front of them, the top of his head shot off.

"A monkey," said Hawke. "It's a damned monkey."

Callender began to laugh, and Hawke pulled him to his feet as lightning flickered.

"Get those muskets ready!" Hawke barked as thunder crashed. "They've heard us now. Get over behind those rocks! Move!"

The jungle was suddenly silent except for the splattering of the rain and the muddy slap of footsteps as the soldiers took new cover. The singing stopped, and the lights in the shrine went black. Huddled behind a stone, Hawke heard the sound of his own heavy breathing and was reassured to find that it hadn't stopped.

"Imagine sending a monkey out like that," he said. "The conniving swine."

"They didn't have to send him out," said Callender. "He was as scared of what's going on in there as you are. It's not natural."

For a moment it seemed as though the singing might start up again, but only a single voice took up the chant, the mystic syllables increasing in volume and ferocity.

"Good God," said Hawke. "What's that?"

The lightning showed him. A lone man, armed only with a sword, stood on the distant steps and roared into the rain. He ran toward the rocks as if he intended to take on Hawke's whole party single-handedly. Hawke was too startled to respond, and perhaps a little nervous about making another mistake, but his men's muskets fired all around him, and through the smoke and falling water he saw the solitary foe twitch and flail and drop. The fusillade had been more than sufficient; Hawke doubted if a single one of the muskets behind him was still loaded.

"Reload!" he shouted.

"They must have all gone mad in there," said Callender. "What could have caused it?"

"Hashish," said Hawke.

"Newcastle," Callender corrected him.

"Kali," murmured the soldiers.

The next symptom of the undiagnosed insanity appeared almost at once when another voice took up the chant. The sound seemed to come from everywhere, but Hawke could not locate its source. He thought he saw shadows moving around the temple, and he fired three shots without result. The devilish song went on. Hawke shivered, and told himself it was the rain.

A distant flash made the sky glow, and in its brief glimmer Hawke saw the man. His jaw dropped. Somehow an inspired Thug had climbed to the very top of the shrine, and there he sat, waving a wet handkerchief as if his only goal in life was to draw fire. If so, he got his wish. He swayed for an instant against the clouds and then tumbled silently down.

"They're crazier than you are," Hawke told Callender, glancing back just long enough to make sure his men were busy with their ramrods. He was trying to decide whether to wait for the cannon or attack at once; it never occurred to him that these bizarre antics might have represented strategy. He missed his last chance to think things over while his men were reloading.

The hissing of the rain seemed heavier for a moment, and the patter of its falling more pronounced. Hawke heard a groan and whipped his head around. Two of his men were down, and the ground was feathered with arrows. Invisible in the downpour, and guided by the flashing of the musket fire, a rain of death had descended on the 5th Fusiliers. Two Thugs had provided the distractions that got the archers into place, and now Hawke and his men were pinned down.

Hawke's shock took the form of disdain. Incredulous,

he raised his head above the rocks. "Arrows," he gasped. "It's like the Dark Ages. Bloody niggers."

Callender, who was surprised to see Hawke sit down abruptly in the mud, was laughing again before he noticed that a wooden shaft was stuck in Hawke's forehead, its point emerging from the back of his skull.

Callender's first thought was that he had never realized an arrow could fly with so much force. His second was that he would soon be as dead as Hawke, who slumped back awkwardly and lay still. Rain fell in his open mouth, and his monocle slipped into the mud.

Callender lay beside the corpse while another volley of arrows rattled down, one of them landing a few inches from his face. One of the soldiers took a shaft in the shoulder, and the others were clearly ready to run. On a rogue mission, without an officer, they would have been daft to stay.

Callender scrambled for Hawke's gun. He hugged the rocks and fired a shot over the heads of the soldiers. His best guess was that it was the last bullet in the revolver. "Get over here by me," he said, clutching the pistol in both his manacled hands.

With a queasy sense of strength he watched them obey his order. They could have killed him in a second, but they were well trained. He saw the power of being English, and it made him slightly sick. He should have let the soldiers run; he should have run with them, but he would be helpless in the jungle with his chains, or even without them. He no longer cared about Newcastle, no longer believed the monster could be slain. It didn't matter. Callender's life was in danger, and Hawke was safely out of it.

"You bastard!" he rasped at Hawke. He took the pistol and smashed its butt repeatedly into the corpse's face. The end of the arrow snapped off, and it was not the only thing that broke.

When Callender was finished, he was amazed to find the soldiers gathered around him. He had been lost in a frenzy, and there had been time for them to escape, but they had stayed. One of them patted him on the back, smiling and nodding his head.

"Spread out," said Callender to his new recruits. "They have our range here. Wait for the lightning, and if you see anyone with a bow, then shoot."

The men scattered into the jungle, and Callender realized that they intended to stick by him. Arrows dropped out of the sky and struck the rocks, but nobody was hiding there. Callender stood behind a tree, his gun empty and his hands bound. A jagged line of blue-white lit the landscape, displaying the archers huddled near Kali's shrine. Callender's men peppered them with lead, then hurried into new positions.

Callender had forgotten about the cannon and took no notice when the trumpet of an elephant sounded through the jungle.

Kalidas Sen ignored the sound as well. He had waited for hours, to be sure it was safe, before approaching the shrine to examine the handiwork of the ghoul he had summoned, but gunfire had greeted him. Now he was perched in the branches of a tree, watching in complete confusion as a battle raged. He could not see the ghoul, or Sebastian, or even Sarala, and he had no idea what was going on, but he had the impression that his band of Thugs had taken on the British Army, and the idea delighted him. Perhaps Sebastian Newcastle had been right, after all. The former leader of the Thugs was filled with pride at the courage of his men, and filled with hatred for the bedraggled stranger who had taken command of the opposing force.

Kalidas Sen wished he had a gun. He wished he had a home. He wished he could be in the shrine. He wished he could be on the moon. His caution kept him safely out of the fray, but his inactivity was driving him into a frenzy.

He was not the only lunatic at large in the monsoon.

Callender rushed from tree to tree as if he could outrun an arrow, but in fact, none was aimed at him, because his empty gun could not provide the burst of fire that might have served as a target.

He was so distraught that it would have taken something the size of a building to get his attention, and that was precisely what arrived.

An elephant thundered out of the trees beyond the shrine, its thick hide glistening in the rain. Callender could barely see the creature through the downpour, but when he heard gunfire crackling from its direction, he knew what it meant. "Hawke's cannon," he whispered.

The sight of the elephant rattled the Thug archers, and the hail of bullets that accompanied it finally broke their nerve. They unloosed another flight of arrows and then bolted for the shelter of the shrine. Two of them died on the steps.

Callender surveyed the area rapidly and began to run toward his reinforcements; if he had not slipped in the mud, he would have been killed by the very men he meant to welcome.

"Don't shoot!" he yelled as bullets whined over his head. "I'm English!"

Callender staggered toward his saviors, only half aware of the odd impression he made: a ragged madman covered with filth and bound in chains. A stocky sergeant, clean-shaven and sunburned, jumped off his horse and held up his hand. "Who the hell are you?" he barked. "Where's Lieutenant Hawke?"

"Hawke's dead, and so are half his men. That place is filled with Thugs, and they've gone mad. You have the cannon?"

"As you see, sir." The sergeant stepped aside, revealing the huge gun behind him. "Just as ordered. And don't think it was easy getting my elephant to pull it though this jungle. Are you sure the lieutenant's dead, sir? Not just wounded, is he?"

"I tell you he's dead, and you'll be too if you don't get that cannon working. You don't know what's going on here!"

"That's right, sir. I don't. And who might you be, sir, if you don't mind me asking?"

"I'm the man those Thugs are trying to kill!"

"I see. You look like some kind of prisoner," observed the sergeant. "Thugs had you, did they?"

"The Thugs?" stuttered Callender, who could never have concocted such a story in his current condition but still had the sense to see the merit in it. "That's right. They were holding me for ransom, and Hawke came here to rescue me. I managed to escape during the fight. I'm a shareholder in the East India Company, and if you know what's good for you, you'll fire on that heathen shrine at once."

"It's true, Sergeant," said a young soldier as he trotted up. "Hawke's dead, all right. His face all battered in."

"Now will you believe me?" demanded Callender, and as he did, the chanting began again.

"What's that?" the sergeant asked.

"That's what they do to work themselves up before they attack. If you don't use the cannon, you'll lose some of these men, and you'll answer to the Company for it!"

"I'll take you at your word, sir. Sergeant Jarvis of the 5th Fusiliers at your service."

"Then shoot, damn it!" bellowed Callender.

"Just as you say, sir. And afterward you'll come back to Dum Dum with us so we can straighten all this out."

Callender saw that it was useless to protest, and in any case he could think of nothing but killing the Thugs before they attacked again. The fever of battle raged through him, and the ungodly song from the shrine was loud in his ears.

"Tell them to get it loaded and ready," Jarvis said to his young messenger.

"And be quick about it!" added Callender.

Jarvis peered through the rain as the doorway of the shrine started to glow again. "That's no Christian place, is it?" he said. "Still, I suppose we should give 'em a fair chance."

"Are you insane?" wailed Callender.

"I don't think so, sir," said Sergeant Jarvis.

He turned and shouted at the shrine with a voice as loud and harsh as only a sergeant's could be. "You in there! Throw down your weapons and come out at once! Come out or we'll blow you all to hell!"

The only reply was the continuation of the eerie melody, rising in pitch and volume as the light from the door turned a blinding white. "I don't think they heard me," Jarvis said.

"They never will," Callender replied. Thunder rumbled in the distance, and a group of men appeared at the incandescent entrance to Kali's shrine.

"You see?" said Jarvis. "They're coming out."

"Not to surrender!" Callender threw himself on the sergeant and knocked him to the ground as the arrows of the Thugs sang through the trees. A man near the cannon screamed and fell; the elephant gave a little shake like someone brushing off a troublesome insect.

"All right," the sergeant roared. "All right! You men at the cannon! Fire!"

Callender clapped his hands over his ears, the chain between his wrists catching him in the face, as the twenty-four pounder roared. He lifted his head out of the mud as if he might have had a chance to watch the iron ball fly through the air, but he was satisfied enough to see its impact on the ancient masonry.

A portion of the wall shattered, just a few feet above the ground, and for an instant white light poured through the gap, then suddenly the whole jungle was illuminated by a scarlet blast. An explosion such as he had never heard knocked Callender backward, and the conelike structure of the shrine seemed to rise in the air as it was torn apart. The broken bodies of men danced in the fireball, and clouds of smoke joined the rain clouds in the sky. Bits of shattered stone and upturned earth rained down on the cannon's crew, and tons of rubble buried the golden statue of Kali. The cannonball had found Kalidas Sen's gunpowder.

Sergeant Jarvis could only sit and stare stupidly at the wreckage that had been a fortress only seconds before. "We couldn't have done that," he said. "There must have been something in there."

Kalidas Sen knew what it was, and when he realized what his false gift to the goddess had accomplished, he became utterly insane. The explosion was so tremendous, its devastation so complete, that it might even have destroyed Sebastian Newcastle, but what did that matter now? The silk merchant had lost everything but the single piece of strong white silk he carried with him, the one he had sworn to use against the enemies of his goddess. He knotted a silver coin in its corner, and stared with burning hatred at the man he had decided to blame for all this night's calamities.

Huddled in the rain, his gaze fixed on the ruin of Kali's shrine, Callender experienced a vague feeling of uneasiness. But if he imagined that somewhere in the jungle there were eyes watching him, he thought only of the dead man he had hounded halfway around the world.

He had never even heard of Kalidas Sen.

## SEVENTEEN

# The Survivors

The rain diminished to a drizzle as the night wore on. Soldiers with lanterns wandered through the ruins of the shrine, calling occasionally to each other as they came across another corpse, or at least part of one. A few of them were playing a little game, quite without their sergeant's knowledge, by trying to put together a whole man out of the pieces they found in the rubble.

Callender walked alone, stirring up debris with his hog spear, looking halfheartedly for some trace of Sebastian or Sarala. The bodies he discovered were not the ones he sought, only dead Thugs with their clothes burned off, their flesh blackened and blistered. A few had been crushed by chunks of falling stone, and here and there a piece of statuary had survived, but these were only corpses of another kind.

"There's a woman over here!" somebody shouted, but when Callender hurried over, he saw that it was only a tone sculpture, and if it held any interest for him at all, that was only because the beautiful nude body and the enigmatic face reminded him of Sarala.

Sergeant Jarvis approached him. "Quite a sight, isn't it?" he said.

Callender looked up from his reverie. "I beg your pardon? Oh. You mean the temple."

"That's right, sir. They must have had an arsenal in here, to make the place blow up this way. I wish I could have had a look inside before it all went up."

"That might have cost you your life, Sergeant."

"True enough. From what we saw, I think it might even have cost me my soul."

The sergeant's messenger hurried up to him, moving deftly through the wreckage without a false step. "Excuse me, Sergeant," he said. "I don't like to interrupt, but there's something strange over there."

"Something strange? What's that?"

"I don't like to say, but it seems like it might be a sort of voice."

"What sort of voice?" demanded Callender.

"Like it was coming from someone buried under these rocks."

"Nonsense," said Sergeant Jarvis. "No one could have lived through that explosion."

"That's what I said. My very words, in fact. But like I told you, there's this sort of voice."

"All right," said Jarvis. "We'll have a look."

Drenched, exhausted, beaten, still shaken by his danger, and never really sane, Callender was nevertheless suddenly eager for action when he heard the man's report. He had no doubt about what was making noises beneath the ruins. What else could have survived? Clutching his spear, he kept in step behind Jarvis as the sergeant made his way to what had been the center of the shrine. Several men were already clearing away the debris, and one of them held a lantern aloft in the thin rain.

Callender crowded forward, and was rewarded with the sound of a faint murmur that might have come from something alive. If it did not sound like Newcastle, Callender remained convinced it could hardly be anyone else. Yet even the idea of making a mistake turned his stomach to stone: a trick had caused Callender to kill his own fiancée in London many months ago, and that was what had brought him here.

"Give us a hand, sir, will you?" Sergeant Jarvis said.

Callender raised his arms and shook the chain between them so that it rattled.

"Sorry, sir. I'd almost forgotten about that. We'll get the regimental blacksmith to take them off as soon as we're back home. It wouldn't do to try shooting 'em off, you see. Might be a ricochet. Don't let it worry you, though. We'll have you looking like a gent again before you see your friends at the East India Company."

Callender had every reason to suspect that things would not work out nearly so pleasantly, but for now his main concern was the pile of stone and timber on the ground. He watched intently as Jarvis joined the others in attempting to dislodge a heavy fragment of rock that seemed to be holding several jagged beams of wood in place. Perhaps, Callender thought, it was the menace of the broken wood that kept the vampire trapped.

The rock tumbled away, and as the soldiers shifted the planks, Callender lifted the spear above his head. One downward stroke would bring him his revenge.

"By God!" said Jarvis. "There is somebody there."

Callender stepped forward to deliver the fatal blow and then stopped short at the sight of what was lying there.

The face he saw was Sarala's.

"She's moving," Jarvis gasped. "She's alive."

Callender was not so sure. Her golden skin was now almost gray, and the eyes she turned on him were as deep and distant as the sky.

He stood frozen in time and space, the spear still poised to plunge into her heart. He knew what she was.

Yet he did not want to see her pierced and did not want to hear her scream. He stared into her steady eyes, and slowly he lowered the spear. Whatever she had become, whatever she might do, he would not cause her further pain.

"I know this woman, Sergeant," he whispered hoarsely. "She was working for Lieutenant Hawke, informing on the Thugs. They must have captured her too."

"Are you badly hurt, ma'am?" asked Jarvis as Sarala raised her head.

Sarala looked at Callender. "It seems strange," she said, "but apparently no harm has been done to me. Thank you."

"We'll get you back to a doctor before you know it," Jarvis told her.

"No," said Sarala. "I cannot stay." To the sergeant's astonishment, she pulled herself to her feet and took a step toward him.

"Let her go, Sergeant," said Callender.

"Go, sir? Where could she go? We're in the middle of the woods here."

"She'll be fine, Sergeant. This is her country, and she has work to do."

"Is that right, ma'am? You're sure you'll be safe?"

Sarala nodded. Her eyes seemed to bore into Jarvis. "Let me go," she said.

"Well, then, I won't make any more trouble for a lady,"

Jarvis said. "I've got enough on my hands already, if yo
don't mind me saying so."

Sarala inclined her head to the sergeant, favored Ca
lender with just the slightest of smiles, and glided towar
the trees. An instant later she had disappeared.

Callender could only guess at what he might have ur
leashed upon the world, yet he was happy to see Saral
escape. He was sick of butchery, and content for now t
avoid more of it regardless of the cost. He felt quite dizzy
and his knees had turned to mush.

"What is it, sir?" the sergeant asked. "Are you al
right?"

Callender swayed and took a clumsy step sideways. "I'r
not quite myself, to tell you the truth."

"That's often the way, sir, after a fight. A man can b
a proper hero when it's called for, and then it catches u
with him all at once when everything's been done. Mayb
you should sit down for a while."

"Thank you, Sergeant. I think I'll feel better if I ca
get away from all these bodies for a few minutes."

"Just as you say, sir. They don't smell good, do they?"

Leaning on his spear, Callender shuffled away from th
shrine, away from Sarala, away from everything. He wa
hollow inside, more tired than he had ever been, and if h
could have slept, he might have wished never to wake u
again.

He made his way into the jungle, finding peace in sol
itude and in the quiet drip of water on the leaves. He sa
slumped forward on a rock, his head hanging, his hand
dangling between his bended knees. He wondered vaguely
about Newcastle, but he could not concentrate. If the vam
pire had vanished, perhaps that was all for the best. In hi
present state of mind, Callender could almost imagine
abandoning his enemy and seeking a new existence fo

210

himself, even if he could hardly imagine what that might be. Unless he took steps quickly, he might end up spending the rest of his days in one of Calcutta's prisons. And if that proved to be worse than a madhouse in London, at least he had experienced an adventure he could never have imagined. He smiled to himself and thought of Sarala. His eyes closed. The soft rain pattered down.

And then his head was jerked back with a wrench that nearly broke his neck.

Something was tugging at his throat, choking off his air, and crushing his windpipe. He tried to reach for it and found his hands entangled in their chain; his fingers could only dig at the silken band embedded in his flesh. He realized as the world went black that he wanted very much to stay alive.

He was only a breath away from asphyxiation when all at once air rushed into his lungs again. Something warm and wet splashed over him, as if the rain had heated and congealed, and then a weight dropped into his lap. Callender looked down at it with bleary eyes and saw the severed head of a Hindu staring up at him, its lips still twitching. He did not recognize the face.

Callender realized that he was covered with the man's fresh blood, and then he toppled over to the ground. A flicker of distant lightning showed him the headless body still standing erect, its bulk supported by two strong white hands. Sebastian Newcastle was feeding at the stump.

Callender's stomach heaved. His vomit choked him as surely as Kalidas Sen's silk handkerchief, and not until it lay mixed in a puddle with the mud did he think to reach for his spear.

Sebastian Newcastle held the weapon in his hands. With a cold glance at Callender, he sent it flying in a long, high arc that seemed to reach into the clouds. Rain washed the thick gouts of blood from his face as he turned it toward Callender.

"This was the king of the Thugs," he said as he kicked the head aside.

"You could have let him kill me," Callender gasped.

"I chose not to."

"You wanted to do it yourself."

"What becomes of you does not concern me, Mr. Callender, but you have done me a service."

"Not willingly," snarled Callender.

"I think you did. You spared the woman known as Sarala."

Thunder rolled, and for a moment Callender was silent. He realized that his life was in this monster's hands, and yet he could not keep his defiance in check. It was as if contact with what he hated gave him strength. He struggled up until he stood face-to-face with the dead man.

"And what is Sarala to you?" asked Callender.

"Less to me than she is to India."

"But you killed her!"

"I set her free."

"And now I suppose you intend to do me the same favor?"

"I have done enough for you tonight. If you wish to die, the river is near at hand. And there, if you wish to live, you will find the boat you came in."

"And where will I go in it?"

"Go home, Callender."

"Go home to what? I have no home! All I have is you!"

Callender was so agitated that he inadvertently reached out to touch Sebastian's arm. The dead man stared at him. "Then perhaps we are brothers," Sebastian said.

Callender withdrew his hand at once, but it was nonetheless quite chilled. "I am no brother of yours," he said. "I am alive!"

"Remember that, then, and remember that I gave your life to you."

"And you destroyed it months ago!"

"If I did," Sebastian said quietly, "then I have returned what I took from you. Our debts are paid."

"I'll call it even when I see you rot."

Sebastian rested his icy fingers on Callender's raw throat. "If you are wise," he said, "you will not see me again at all."

"Going to run away again, are you? Going to leave me here in chains to explain all this to the East India Company?"

"There is no place for me in India now," Sebastian said.

"And you expect me to let you run free?"

Sebastian grasped Callender's wrists and pulled him forward until Callender could see nothing but the fathomless darkness of the dead man's eyes.

"You speak to me of freedom?" Sebastian roared.

Callender felt pressure on his wrists and heard the sound of metal snapping. When he looked down, his manacles were gone. And then Sebastian knocked him down into the puddle of his own vomit.

"Now, Mr. Callender, you have more freedom than I shall ever know."

Sebastian walked away, and as he did Callender noticed that his left foot dragged behind him. The limp put Callender in mind of someone else, and clearly the vampire absorbed this thought at once, for he turned toward Callender once again, only his pale face visible now among the trees.

"Where is the boy?" he called out.

"At Dum Dum," said Callender.

"And is he safe?"

"Safe in prison."

Sebastian dropped back into the darkness. Yet even after he was gone, his presence still remained, in whispered words that might have been no more than the hissing of the rain.

"Forget me, Callender, for your own sake."

Callender lay in the rain for what seemed like a long time, but finally he remembered that the soldiers were not far away and might be looking for him soon.

He got up and began to walk toward the river.

# EIGHTEEN

# The Boy in the Cage

The next night found Jamini still locked in his cell in the guardhouse at Dum Dum. He was grateful to have gone so long without receiving a visit from Lieutenant Hawke, but he would have been somewhat less satisfied with his lot if he had realized that nobody in authority even knew he was a prisoner, and he was consequently unlikely ever to be released.

The steady downpour outside the prison soothed him, and he slept as much as he could. There was nothing else to do but feel the painful throbbing of his foot.

He was bored and hungry, and just starting to be afraid that he would be left alone forever, when he heard a key turn in the lock and saw the door swing slowly open.

His own demon stood on the threshold.

"Sebastian!" the boy whispered. "I knew you would come."

"Are you hurt, boy?"

"That Englishman broke my foot."

"The one called Callender?"

"The other one. The soldier. I'd like to kill him."

"He is already dead."

"Did you do it, Sebastian?"

"No. It was one of the Thugs."

Jamini smiled. "And now you have come to take me out of here," he said. "Have you killed all the guards?"

"Not a single one," Sebastian said.

"Then you used magic?"

"I used a bribe," Sebastian told him.

Jamini looked at his demon with disappointment in his eyes.

"Gold can be a useful thing," Sebastian said. "Can you walk, boy?"

"I can limp."

"Then we will limp together. I have been wounded too."

Sebastian hobbled into the cell and reached out his hand. Jamini stared at him, utterly dismayed.

"But how could you be hurt? I told the English where you were because I knew you would kill them all, but I never thought they could hurt you!"

"Perhaps I will be healed, in time. Perhaps both of us will be healed."

"I think I might be lame forever, unless you help me with your magic."

"I have no magic for that, Jamini. You will have to find a doctor. Come on, now. We must leave this place. Lean on me."

The two of them made their way down the narrow corridor and out into the night. The guards they passed stared straight ahead as if no one was there, but one of them winked at the boy. Jamini was disgusted.

216

"How could you give them money?" he whispered as they stepped into the rain. "We should be fighting them. We should fight them until they all go home!"

"Perhaps there will be fighting soon," Sebastian said, "unless India means to let the English rule forever."

"Why don't they just go away, Sebastian?"

"I never heard of conquerors who realized they were wrong. It is not the way of men."

They walked in silence for some time, Jamini taking pleasure in the sight of the sky, the touch of raindrops on his face, and the companion who walked by his side. Sebastian's mood troubled him, but that would pass, and then they would see more wonders together.

When they reached the outskirts of Calcutta, Sebastian stopped and pressed something into Jamini's palm. The boy opened his hand and found in it a finger made of gold.

"This is from the goddess," Jamini said. "From Kali!"

"You must forget about that," Sebastian said. "It is only a piece of gold. Use it to keep yourself alive, and forget about the goddess. Put your faith in gold, or love, or war, or anything you choose, but never put your faith in magic, for it will betray you."

The boy stood with his hand outstretched as if he could not understand what the gift meant. He knew, but he would not admit it to himself. "But you are magic," he said to Sebastian, "and you would never betray me."

"You see how wrong you are to believe in such things? This is the last you will see of me, Jamini."

The boy's eyes smarted. "But then why did you set me free?"

"Everyone should be free, Jamini, but you will not be truly free until you have forgotten Sebastian."

"But what will I do?"

"Take the gold and use it." Sebastian's voice was turning harsh. "Apprentice yourself. Take up a trade. Learn to live like other men."

The boy clenched his fist around the golden finger. "I will learn to fight and kill," he said.

Sebastian looked at the boy as if seeing him for the first time. "Then would you be a Thug, Jamini?"

"No. The Thugs are wrong. They kill anyone, but I will kill only the English."

The boy might have said more, but when he lifted up his eyes to face Sebastian, Jamini realized that he was alone. The street was empty and his friend was gone. In his place there was only a ribbon of mist, and that was soon washed away by falling rain.